# Hypnotism in Victorian and Edwardian Era Fiction
## Volume III.

# The Hypnotic Tales

of

# Rafael Sabatini

Edited by

## Donald K. Hartman

## THEMES & SETTINGS IN FICTION PRESS

Buffalo, New York

# THEMES & SETTINGS IN FICTION PRESS

Buffalo, New York

First Edition, 2024

Layout by
David J. Bertuca

Original cover artwork by
Laura Schmitz Lubniewski

**Publisher's Cataloging-in-Publication Data**

Names: Hartman, Donald K., editor | Sabatini, Rafael
Title: The Hypnotic Tales of Rafael Sabatini / edited by Donald K.
Hartman.
Series: Hypnotism in Victorian and Edwardian era fiction ; 3
Description: First Edition. | Buffalo, N.Y. : Themes & Settings in
Fiction Press, 2024. | Includes bibliographical references.
Summary: Two stories on hypnotism by Rafael Sabatini, plus
biographical background on the author.
Contents: Introduction — Background Information on Trilby —
The Avenger — The Dream — Review of The Recoil: a Film
Adaptation of The Dream.
Identifiers: Library of Congress Control Number: 2023944164 |
ISBN 9780960082322 (print)
Subjects: LCSH: Hypnotism and crime—Fiction. | Hypnotism
in literature. | Mesmerism in literature. | Animal magnetism—
Fiction. | Murder—Fiction.
Classification: LCC *PN6071.H9 H765 2024* | *DDC 813.08 H765--*
dc23

# Contents

Introduction ................................................................. v

Background Information on *Trilby* ............................... vii

The Avenger ................................................................. 1

The Dream ............................................................... 89

Review of The Recoil: a film adaptation of The Dream 153

# Introduction

Today, few people would recognize the name *Rafael Sabatini*, but in the 1920s and 1930s he was one of the most popular authors in the world. Called "the Alexandre Dumas of Modern Fiction" and "the Prince of Storytellers," he almost single-handedly resurrected the genre of the swashbuckler in both literature and film. Sabatini was a master of adventure tales, and his stories would have a major influence on the portrayal of pirates in Hollywood films for several decades (Tyrone Power and Errol Flynn both starred in movie versions of his seafaring novels). Born in Italy in 1875, Sabatini was the son of an English mother and an Italian father, both of whom were professional opera singers. Rafael was educated in schools in Switzerland and Portugal, and at the age of 17, he moved with his parents to Liverpool, England. Sabatini had a natural proclivity for languages, a skill that enabled him to obtain a job as a translator of business documents for an import company specializing in trading Brazilian goods. During the time he was working for the import firm he began to realize that his real interest was in becoming a writer. A couple of years after his arrival in Liverpool Rafael began to write stories for his own enjoyment, and at one point he showed some of his stories to a journalist who not only liked the stories but encouraged Sabatini to submit them to an editor the journalist knew. Several of his early stories were published in minor literary periodicals, and Rafael appears to have been surprised that his fictional writings were marketable. Sabatini would spend several years in literary obscurity before he started placing his short stories into large, national magazines, and it was during the period of Sabatini's life when he was on the cusp of global popularity, that he wrote the two tales included in the book in front of you.

Historical romances and adventure stories were Sabatini's stock-in-trade and the focal point of the majority of his literary writings, but for a brief time, at the beginning of his writing career, he must have had at least a passing interest in hypnotism, for he would write, not one, but two stories dealing with the subject. The first of his hypnotic tales was *The Avenger*, which appeared in the March 1909 issue of *Gunter's Magazine*. In *The Avenger,* we meet Roger Galliphant, a man with medical training and a strong interest in psychology and psychic research. Galliphant is also a powerful hypnotist who, while performing a simple demonstration of hypnotism in front of friends, discovers that an acquaintance of his, James Chester, has used hypnotism to commit at least two murders. Roger Galliphant, knowing the difficulty of proving Chester's crimes in a court of law, plans on avenging the murder victims' deaths, and he does so by using his own hypnotic powers against those of Chester's—and thus a battle between hypnotists ensues. Roger Galliphant also appears in Sabatini's second tale dealing with hypnosis, *The Dream*, a novelette published in the August 1912 issue of *The Story-Teller*. Galliphant appears toward the end of the story when he is needed as an eminent authority on hypnotism, and he must decide if Francis Orpington was under the influence of hypnotic suggestion when he killed an unarmed man.

# Background Information on *Trilby*

[The opening chapter of *The Avenger*, has three of the story's main characters talking about the validity of hypnotism, a discussion initiated by them having just seen a stage version of the popular novel, *Trilby*, at the Haymarket Theatre in London.]

Few books have attained the popularity of George du Maurier's novel, *Trilby*. One of the most successful novels of the nineteenth century, it was first published serially in *Harper's Monthly* in 1894, and then in book form in 1895, and it sold over 200,000 copies in its first year. Many books have sold as well or better than *Trilby*, but few have captivated the public imagination to the same degree. *Trilby* was not just a publishing and literary phenomenon; it created a mania, referred to at the time as "Trilbyana." The Trilby craze appears to have influenced all levels of daily life, from products tied to the novel, such as dolls, toys, board games, shoe polish, soap, and toothpaste, to food-related items such as sausage, ham, candy and cocktails. The stage version of *Trilby* also had an effect on fashion with the creation of the "Trilby," a narrow-brimmed type of hat worn by one of the characters in the play. One of the curiosities that sprung from the novel and its theatre renditions was an obsession with the eponymous heroine's feet—Trilby's feet are described as "astonishingly beautiful feet" in the novel, and the stage versions of the story would prominently highlight Trilby's bare feet. The Trilby foot fetish would lead to a style of high-heeled shoe, and to many odd commercial products including foot-shaped Trilby ice cream and silver scarf pins modelled on her feet. Trilbyana would extend into the realm of geography when the town of Macon in Florida would rename itself as "Trilby" in 1895.

*Trilby* is set in mid-nineteenth century bohemian Paris. Trilby O'Ferrall, the novel's heroine, is laundress and artist model in the Latin Quarter of the city. She is friends with three artists: "Taffy" Wynne, Sandy McAlister, and "Little Billee" Bagot, a painter, whose drawing of Trilby's beautiful foot is a masterpiece. Little Billee loves Trilby, and she returns the feeling, but Billee's family oppose the match, so Trilby decides to refuse Little Billee's proposal. Among the people who frequent the artists' studio is Svengali, an Austrian Jew, who is a repugnant but gifted musician. Trilby falls under the spell of the compelling Svengali, and he trains her singing voice through hypnotism and turns her into a diva. Svengali, through the use of his mesmeric powers, forces Trilby to go away with him. After their escape from Paris, the pair travel throughout Europe on a successful concert tour—Trilby winning fame as a concert performer, always singing in a kind of hypnotic trance under Svengali's influence. Svengali dies suddenly at a concert while Trilby is singing; upon his death, their hypnotic connection is broken, and Trilby loses her power to sing, she goes into physical decline and dies.

*Trilby* was adapted into several long-running plays in both England and the United States, and it also had several film adaptations (these were often titled "Svengali"), as silent films in 1912, 1914, 1915, 1923 and 1927, and "talkies" in 1931 and 1954; a TV movie starring Jodie

Foster and Peter O'Toole appeared in 1983. Today, *Trilby* has fallen into relative obscurity. The main reason for this is the book's antisemitism and its depiction of the Jewish Svengali as an evil figure with pointed ears, a beard, and a hooked nose. Another reason could be the novel's writing style that frequently shifts between English and French and other languages which could create a stumbling block for English-language-only readers. While *Trilby* has fallen out of favor, the word "Svengali" has entered into common parlance, meaning a person who completely dominates another, usually with selfish or sinister motives. In the courtroom, the "Svengali defense" is a legal tactic that portrays the defendant as a pawn of a larger and more influential criminal mastermind.

Suggested readings on *Trilby*:

The novel itself is copyright free, and widely available on the Internet via:

Project Gutenberg
https://www.gutenberg.org/ebooks/39858

The Internet Archive
https://archive.org/details/trilbynovel00dumaiala

HathiTrust
https://catalog.hathitrust.org/Record/001023656

*Trilbyana: The Rise and Progress of a Popular Novel.* New York: Critic Co., 1895.

Jenkins, Emily. "Trilby Fads, Photographers, and Over-Perfect Feet." *Book History* Vol. 1 (1998), pp. 221-267.

Purcell, L. Edward. "Trilby and Trilby-Mania: The Beginning of the Bestseller System." *Journal of Popular Culture* Vol. 11 (Summer 1977): pp.62-76.

Ferguson, Christine. "Footnotes on *Trilby*: The Human Foot as Evolutionary Icon in Late Victorian Culture." *Nineteenth-Century Contexts* Vol. 28 (2006): pp.127-144.

Haugtvedt, Erica. "Trilby-Mania: Serial Fiction Merchandising During the Fin de siècle."

(Blog post on RSVP – The Research Society for Victorian Periodicals) URL: https://rs4vp.org/trilby-mania-by-erica-haugtvedt-ohio-state-university/

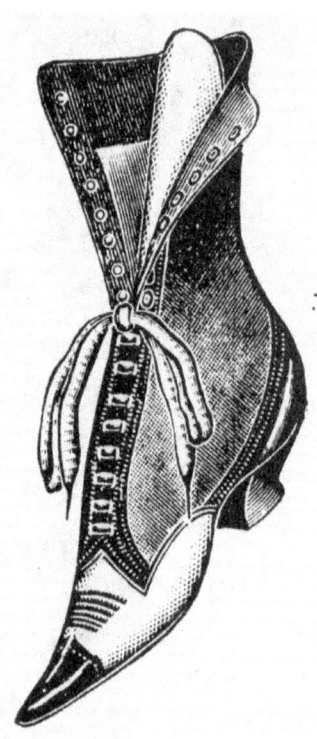

## The Trilby.

(Weight, 15 ounces.)

52068   The very latest in ladies' footwear. cloth top fine dongola foxing. Picadilly last. The toe is long and pointed, with long patent leather tip and corded vamp, turn sole and medium low heel; it also has a fancy patent leather stay up the front, which makes the lacing flies more durable, and also adds to the general appearance of the shoe for dress or street wear. There is nothing finer. We can recommend this shoe for fair and reasonable service. Sizes, 2½ to 7. Widths, C, D, E, and EE. Per pair ............$2.75

# The Avenger

It was late one summer night—or, rather, very early one summer morning—that we stumbled upon the discovery of that awful crime. And the manner of that discovery will serve as a further instance of the overwhelming effects that are at times to be obtained from the most trivial causes.

Voysey had taken Galliphant and me to his rooms in Maddox Street for a pipe and a final chat before separating.

We had been celebrating Voysey's home-coming. We had dined together—and very choicely—and we had afterward gone to The Haymarket, where "Trilby" was drawing all London at the time. Upon this—upon the circumstance that it was to "Trilby" that we went, and not to any other of the plays then running—hangs the whole sequence of astounding happenings that followed.

But first let me tell you of Voysey and of the events that led to that trip of his round the world from which he was freshly returned. Of course there was a woman in the story; in fact, there were two women, and one of them—Pauline Cornaby—was, I think, the sweetest and most desirable girl it has ever been my lot to meet; the other was Miss Cornaby's mother.

I wish as far as possible to hold the scales impartially, as is the duty of every honest chronicler, but the desire to be impartial leaves me at a loss to know whether to invite your pity or your scorn for Mrs. Cornaby. She was a worldly, selfish woman, and for that she deserves to be contemned; but she was also an exceedingly foolish woman, who had not the power to see things as they are; and when we consider that her worldliness, her selfishness, her vanity and what other faults she had, sprang from mental obtuseness and sheer stupidity, it becomes necessary to temper our contempt with pity.

Usually these attributes make for comedy. But in Mrs. Cornaby's case the ends they achieved leave us aghast at the potentialities for tragedy that lie occasionally within the compass of a silly woman.

Frank Voysey had come to love Miss Cornaby with all the strength of his fine nature when Colin Chester, in utter ignorance of his friend's feelings, came upon the scene. Chester was wealthy; so wealthy as to make Voysey's handsome income seem a mere pittance by comparison; and his family was one of the oldest in the country, whereas Frank's father had amassed his fortune in pickles, as everybody knew. From a worldly point of view their positions would not bear comparison; from a moral or intellectual point of view there was little to choose between them; while from the purely animal point of view, Voysey derived a slight advantage from his fair, honest, well-featured face, and clean, athletic length of limb. Mrs. Cornaby's point of view was solely and essentially the worldly. Voysey had commended himself to her as a most desirable son-in-law until Chester appeared. When that happened she set about employing those artifices of cunning with which the stupid are so often gifted—perhaps by way of compensation—to cause Voysey to cease his visits, and to induce her daughter to conclude that she had been mistaken in her estimate of Voysey's character.

Now, Frank Voysey was extremely, almost foolishly, sensitive and humble-minded. It was ever his dread that he might not be wanted; let but the faintest shadow of a hint confirm that dread of his, and he vanished. Knowing him as I do, I realize how much it must have cost him in the case of Pauline Cornaby. Nevertheless, he went, and Pauline's engagement to his friend Colin was announced soon afterward.

It was then that Voysey appeared at his very best. He put behind him his sorrow and his great sense of loss, and he went down to Cheynesworth Towers, that he might in person bear his congratulations and good wishes to this friend of his youth, who so little suspected the inward agony that his own happiness was occasioning Voysey.

Colin urged him to prolong his visit, with the result that he was still at Cheynesworth on that fatal night, a couple of weeks later, when Colin met his death. In a somnambulistic trance the ill-starred young man set out to walk along the summit of a wall of his ancient home, and, missing his footing, fell from a height of nearly fifty feet, and was killed on the spot.

Grief at the tragic end of his friend stifled at first every other consideration in Voysey's mind. Later, however, he had scarcely been human had he not permitted himself to realize that by Colin's decease his own way to Pauline Cornaby was open once more. Natural delicacy, of course, forbade any undue haste in pursuing this; and, so, he waited. But he went down to Marleford a good deal in those days, and Pauline manifested more than a friendly pleasure in his company. Her mother had discovered, and very opportunely confessed to, her mistake concerning Frank.

Meanwhile Robert Chester—Colin's younger brother—had succeeded to the estates, and soon a second tragedy came to deepen the gloom that still hung over Cheynesworth. Robert—a stalwart, healthy youngster of twenty-two—was found dead in his bed one morning, and the doctors pronounced his death to be due to heart-failure.

Again Cheynesworth Towers welcomed a new master. This time it was James Chester, the next of kin, a second cousin of the deceased brothers, a spendthrift who had lived until then mainly on the charity of his cousins.

Some two months after Robert's death, Voysey was at last on the point of putting his fate to the test with Pauline, when he received a letter from Mrs. Cornaby announcing her daughter's engagement to the latest master of Cheynesworth Towers. Frank had been out of England for a month, at the bedside of an ailing sister in Italy, and he found the letter awaiting him on his return.

He took it very badly. To him it meant more than the loss of the woman he loved—he had borne that with some equanimity when she became engaged to Colin—it meant the shattering of an idol. It is a strange thing that a man always takes a blow of this kind worst when the woman who deals it tumbles in the act from the pedestal on which he had placed her, and allows him to behold her in a light which, rather than causing him to grieve over the loss of her, should inspire him with gratitude to the fates that have saved him from being her victim.

Voysey took it so badly that his health was affected, and Galliphant—who acted as his medical adviser— prescribed for him a trip round the world that he might find an anodyne in distraction.

And now he was home again, bronzed and healthy, and apparently in the best of spirits, and as we sat that night in his old rooms in Maddox Street it hardly seemed as if he had ever been away.

Our talk drifted naturally enough to the play we had witnessed. Galliphant was immensely taken with it, and Galliphant was something of a judge of matters literary and artistic. To me "Trilby" had brought that pang of disappointment produced not infrequently by the dramatic version of a book we have immensely admired. The stage has its limitations in the matter of subtlety, whereas the novelist's work is bounded only by the limitations of his own spirit. I was disappointed, and I confessed my disappointment freely. Galliphant disagreed with me, and thereby unwittingly laid the cornerstone to all that followed.

"With me," he said, "the play rendered salient many of the features that in the book I had underestimated."

"While with me it did the very opposite," said I. "It brought out in all its flagrant absurdity that jumble of hypnotic nonsense of the plausibility of which Du Maurier's manner had all but convinced me in the book."

"That jumble of hypnotic nonsense?" Galliphant echoed questioningly, and his keen blue eyes fastened upon me with one of those long steady looks that are a discomposing and hardly courteous habit of Galliphant's. "I should like to argue the point with you if I might have a better notion of what you mean."

"My dear fellow," I laughed, "I am not going to be lured into any argument with you. I have my own ideas about hypnotism."

"And so have I," said Galliphant gravely. "Supposing we compare them."

In many ways Roger Galliphant's was a striking personality. He had about him an air of power and distinction that would detach him in any assembly that he might enter. Although considerably under forty, his thick, wavy hair was almost completely white; the prematureness of this was loudly proclaimed by the keen, bronzed youthful face beneath, clean-shaven, well-featured and free of wrinkles save for the lines that thought had graven on his intelligent brow. His eyes were large and full and of a singularly deep blue, and I have already alluded to the trick they had of riveting themselves upon the eyes of any one with whom he happened to be drawn into serious or contentious conversation. He was a bachelor, and possessed of more than ample means; but to satisfy the wishes of his father who desired him to have a profession in his grasp against a possible day of need, he had graduated in his youth as a bachelor of medicine. But he had never followed it even as a hobby, although his habits were intensely studious. He had elected, however, to go further afield; and making use of his medical training as a basis he had at one time seemed by way of achieving something of a reputation as an evolutionist. Suddenly, however, he abandoned physiology for psychology, and devoted himself for a time to psychic research, only to forsake it shortly after in disgust at the empirics who flourished by it, and convinced by the investigations he had made that further investigations would be a waste of time. He deplored his momentary defection from the philosophy of Haeckel, and let the matter drop. Nor did he willingly refer to it again.

One flower, however, he had culled in the field of his psychic wanderings, and that flower he brought back with him and cultivated until it became the study of his life. That flower—if you will allow an image of whose inadequacy I am aware—was the phenomenon of hypnosis. But he had pursued his studies so secretly that until the night in question I was entirely ignorant of them, or else you may be very sure that I had never ventured to oppose his views with my own.

"Am I correct," he inquired presently, "in assuming your ideas of hypnotism might be summed up into the one word 'humbug'? Is that what you wish to convey by your sneers at the impossibility of *Svengali*?"

"More or less," I answered. "What do you say, Frank?"

"I?" said Voysey, and his face was grave. "I say that you are wrong."

"Of course he's wrong," said Galliphant, "and as obstinate in his error as is usual with the ignorant." He suffered at times from an excess of candor—or, rather, he made others suffer from it.

"I will not believe," I said, "that which I cannot understand."

"How limited, then," said Galliphant in his pleasant way, "must be your field of faith. You have not, I take it, made any serious study of hypnotism?"

"No," I answered frankly. "I know of no studies worth making."

"Yet," he contended, "there is no lack of text-books on the rationale of the subject."

"Nor yet on the subject of psychic research," I retorted, hitting back at last. "You will find men to write on any subject likely to appeal to the weak-minded. They can thus depend upon a large public."

"You are of course quite wrong on the score of hypnotism," he said quietly, sticking to the point, and the finality of his manner staggered me.

"Do you seriously mean," I asked, "that a man of your mental powers can attach belief to the absurdities credited to hypnotism?"

"No," he replied, with a smile, "not to the absurdities. I discard those. But there remain many things in hypnotism that are not absurd."

"Granted," I cried, imagining that I understood his drift. "You must not suppose that I go so far as to deny the existence of hypnotic phenomenon. I acknowledge it, but within the bounds of reason."

"And what may you consider the bounds of reason?"

"Why, I realize that by a fixed stare at some bright object the eyes grow weary, and, as we all know, there is no fatigue so inductive of sleep as the fatigue of the eyes. Thus, I believe that insomnia, for instance, may be combated with success. So far I will acknowledge the state of artificially induced sleep for which the word 'hypnotism' will serve as well as another. But as for any mental link between hypnotizer and hypnotee, as for any influence that the former may be able to exert over the latter, that is a belief that I leave to credulous old ladies. And that is what was in my mind when I described the achievements of *Svengali* as a jumble of absurdities."

Galliphant smiled the smile of the man who, invested with definite and precise knowledge, tolerates contradiction from a child. He turned to Voysey.

"And you, Voysey?" he inquired.

"I am with the credulous old ladies," answered Voysey without smiling.

Galliphant looked at me again. "I should like," he said reflectively, "to convince you of your error."

His seriousness impressed me. My respect for his attainments awoke, now that I realized that our views must be very widely at variance.

"Do you really mean to say that the things that *Svengali* does in 'Trilby' are possible in ordinary life?" I asked.

"I mean," he answered seriously, "that I saw very little that was improbable, and hardly anything that was impossible."

"If you say so," I said, completely defeated, "that is enough for me." And then an idea occurred to me. "Are your conclusions based upon experiment," I asked, "or only upon study? I mean, have you ever practiced hypnotism?"

"A little," he answered modestly.

"Successfully?"

"Why, yes; successfully."

Curiosity got the better of me and excited now my keenest interest in a subject to which hitherto I had been indifferent with the skepticism of the ignorant, and I did not hesitate to confess that I now thirsted for such knowledge and demonstration as should completely convince me.

"You mean," he said, "that you must have ocular proof before you can have faith. You are not unreasonable. That was my own feeling once. Well, you shall have your demonstration at the earliest opportunity."

It must have been Fate, speaking with the voice of my odd impatience, that urged me to reply that no opportunity could be better than the present. The hour was propitious, and I invited him—in my ignorance—to afford me proof by hypnotizing me.

"But, my dear fellow," he remonstrated, "what sort of demonstration do you suppose that would be? You would be conscious of nothing beyond the circumstance that you had slept for a time, and sleep, you know, is the one feature of hypnotism of which you do not need conviction. In a deep hypnosis your memory, your consciousness would be wiped out, and similarly upon awaking you would retain no recollection of anything that had taken place."

But Fate continued to take a hand in the affair, whetting my curiosity and rendering me more and more impatient as Galliphant threw out objections. In the end I said something that suggested to him that I was casting a doubt upon his powers. He was always a shade intolerant of contradiction, particularly from the ill-informed, and he answered me sharply that I should have a demonstration next day, as soon as he could find a willing subject.

It was then that Voysey solved the situation.

"Let him have it now, since he is so eager," he said. "I will be your subject, Roger, and I think that you will find me easy to induce."

Galliphant looked at him, first in surprise, then in consideration.

"Yes," he said slowly, "I should imagine you would be a good subject; you belong to the sensitive type that is readily responsive. From what you say I take it that you have been hypnotized before?"

"Once, by James Chester, at Cheynesworth, a year ago."

"Why?" asked Galliphant.

"I was in poor health, and I submitted to it as a cure to insomnia. Of course the trance induced was a light one; merely sufficient to put me to sleep. But I understand that I proved a singularly sensitive subject, and that a deeper trance might easily have been induced. Anyhow, you can make the experiment if you care to, and so convince Martin."

Galliphant manifested some reluctance, observing which I sought in a half-hearted way to put off the experiment. But Voysey made little of Galliphant's reluctance, and took no notice whatever of my objections, which, no doubt, sounded as insincere as they were.

Suddenly Galliphant gave way. So suddenly that I looked at him. His fine, solemn face was oddly purposeful.

"Very well," he said. "Since you are so extremely amiable about it, Martin shall have his demonstration. Sit Here."

## II.

Expectancy put the last misgiving from my mind as I watched Galliphant making his preparations.

He disposed Voysey in a comfortable armchair, and perched himself upon one of its arms, so that by turning his head to the right his face was brought opposite and fairly close to that of his subject. Next he desired me to switch off the electric lamp that Voysey was facing, so that the only light in the room was behind Frank's head, leaving his features, therefore, more or less in shadow.

"There are, as you may know, Martin," said Galliphant in the tone of a lecturer, "several ways of inducing the hypnotic state. A mirror, or a metal disk, or a ring, or even the operator's finger held thus at a little distance from the subject's eyes, are among the various aids adopted. Myself, however, I dispense with all adjuncts, employing the method known as fascination."

I nodded to signify that I understood, and Galliphant turned to face his subject. Voysey's hands were rested upon his knees, and Galliphant now covered them with his own, bidding Voysey to gaze into his eyes. A couple of minutes went by in utter silence; then, quite suddenly, Voysey drew a breath with a deep, sighing inspiration;

his eyelids flickered, a quiver ran through his body, and a spasm as of laughter—foolish and vacuous—swept across his face.

And now Galliphant was making long, slow, downward passes with his hands. Voysey shuddered again and lay quite still, his breathing deep and regular.

Roger rose and faced me.

"He is an excellent subject," he said quietly, and crossing to the table he took a cigarette from the silver box that stood there.

I said nothing. To tell the truth, I was rather awed by my first acquaintance with hypnotism. Galliphant, with his back to Voysey, struck a match.

"There was not even," he said, "the need of suggestion. He is now in a deep trance. Sense and volition are alike suspended. Presently he shall have no mind but my mind, know no will but my will."

"It is awful," I muttered, and I think I almost shuddered, my skepticism entirely forgotten now in the contemplation of Voysey's strangely altered countenance. All the character seemed to have departed out of it; it looked blank as the face of the dead may look, and it was not difficult to believe that such expression as it might assume should be in answer to the will that had reduced it to its present expressionlessness.

"Yes," answered Galliphant, "it is awful, a terrible power; and in the hands of the criminal or the unscrupulous a power too terrible to be considered calmly." He crushed down the wooden match into the ash-tray as he spoke. "I should never have given way to your urging, and consented to do this," he said gravely, "if it had not occurred to me that I might take advantage of the circumstance to complete in Voysey the cure which his travels have so favored."

"How do you mean?" I asked, in some surprise.

"You shall have full and immediate proof of what it is possible to do, and I think you will agree that the feats of *Svengali* hardly transcend the possible. In addition to that, however, before I wake Voysey from his trance, I propose to make use of post-hypnotic suggestion to cure him of any lingering feeling for Miss Cornaby."

"Can so much be done?"

"I can try—provided that you consider I should be justified."

"I most certainly think so."

"I am very glad, because that is why I consented to this experiment. And now, what tricks shall he perform first of all by way of satisfying you? Like *Trilby* he is singularly lacking in musical accomplishments. He is without ear and without sense of time. Shall he sing for you?"

But I paid no heed to his last question, so impressed and startled was I by the awful change that had gradually spread over Voysey's white face.

"Look!" I cried. "My God! What is happening to him? You've gone too far, Galliphant." And I started to my feet in my excitement.

Galliphant swung round to look at Voysey. The man's countenance was distorted. Its frank youthfulness, its honesty and loftiness of expression had all indeed departed when he sank into that trance. But expression had crept once more into the blank that had been left, and it was horrible to behold. His face had become as the face of a satyr; his lips were drawn down in a sneering smile, singularly, unspeakably wicked. Deep furrows stood between his closed eyes, heightening the horrid stamp of evil on his countenance.

From the subject I glanced now at the operator. He was standing beside Voysey, observing him, a puzzled, almost bewildered look in his eyes. Suddenly they cleared, as if understanding had flashed upon him; he muttered an exclamation under his breath. His glance turned to me an instant, and he seemed on the point of speaking; then he leaned slightly forward toward Voysey, and his voice, calm, deliberate and with a note of singular command, uttered Voysey's name. Instantly the expression of the sleeping man's face changed to one of alertness.

"Yes," he answered, his voice quiet and monotonous. "I hear you."

"What did you see just now, Frank? Of what were you thinking?" Galliphant inquired in the same calm commanding tone. "Answer me."

Again there came a change over Voysey's face. His brows were knit a moment, as if he were in thought; then the furrows deepened, and the horrid sneer crept back to the corners of his mouth.

"I am thinking," he answered, in that mechanical voice, "of Colin Chester and how I killed him that night at Cheynesworth."

That answer—that statement in that cold, deliberate voice, issuing from those lips wreathed in that infernal smile—struck a chill of horror unspeakable through me. But the next moment I realized that I was foolish, that the whole business was foolishness. The mind which Galliphant had boasted should hold no thought but such as he inspired it with, was wandering in a land of dreams and hallucinations as wanders the mind of any man asleep. Indeed it seemed to me a culminating proof that I had been right to hold hypnotism lightly, to refuse to regard it as anything more than a more or less natural sleep artificially induced, and to disdain belief in any of the tricks that are to be seen performed in music-halls by empirics who trade upon the credulity of an ignorant public. It came to me, too, as something of a shock that I should be right and Galliphant wrong. And it surprised me to hear Galliphant still asking questions, which, it seemed to me, could be doing no more than sound the depths of Voysey's bad dream.

"Why did you kill him, Voysey?"

"Because I hated him," came the answer in that same voice of deadly calm. "Because he robbed me of Pauline."

"How did you kill him?"

"I surprised him asleep in bed. I stabbed him where he lay."

Now all of this was preposterous. The manner of Colin's death was not one that admitted of the slightest doubt. Voysey himself and James Chester, besides a gamekeeper in Cheynesworth Park, had seen the poor fellow on the wall in his fit of somnambulism; they had witnessed the terrific fall that broke his neck, and a dozen people had seen him a few moments after, as he still lay where he had fallen. Nor was there any wound about him besides the injuries received in his fall. Why, then, pursue these fruitless questions, and prolong the agony of Voysey's ghastly, hypnotic nightmare? Galliphant's face, moreover, was preternaturally grave; so grave and thoughtful that it provoked from me the expostulation:

"One might almost think that you believe him."

His answer startled me more than all that I had heard or witnessed so far. "I do," he said quietly, "implicitly. He is speaking the truth."

"The truth? Galliphant! What are you saying? We all know how Colin died. Besides Voysey's evidence, there is that of James Chester and that of the gamekeeper."

"Nevertheless," Galliphant repeated solemnly, "he is speaking the truth."

"What on earth can you mean?"

"No more than that. I can offer no explanation. But I have an idea—vague as yet." He broke off; thought a moment; then, with a soft exclamation of discovery, of satisfaction, he turned again to Voysey.

"Do you recollect seeing Colin after you had killed him?" was his fresh question.

Voysey's brows were knit, as if he were making an effort of memory. Then an odd puff of laughter escaped him. "Why, no. That is odd, now!" The furrows deepened a moment.

"Think!" Galliphant commanded him.

There was a pause. Then: "No," said Voysey. "I do not remember seeing him after he was dead."

Galliphant's solemn eyes met mine for a moment. "I think I understand," he said, and stood pondering for some moments.

"What do you understand?" I asked at last, impatiently. But if he heard it, he never heeded my question.

"I am afraid we are to have no other demonstration for you to-night." He said presently. "The time would be too ill-chosen."

But not only did we forego the demonstration. In his present, evidently disturbed state of mind, Galliphant seemed to forget that other and more serious purpose for which he had consented to hypnotize Voysey, for without waiting for more he took him by the shoulder and shook him vigorously.

"Wake up, Voysey!" he commanded in a loud voice, accompanying his words by a few upward passes over the sleeper's face. The deep, regular breathing was checked. Voysey opened his eyes, and looked round in the uncomprehending manner of one suddenly brought from deep slumber to entire wakefulness.

I cannot say now whether it was Galliphant's solemnity that had impressed me, or whether there were other, subtler influences at work; but I do know that I felt strangely perturbed and ill at ease, as if oppressed by a sense of some impending catastrophe.

Memory came quickly back to Voysey, and a smile brightened his face. His frank, honest eyes traveled from me to Galliphant.

"Well?" he began, and then abruptly stopped, checked by something in Galliphant's expression. Questioningly, and growing suddenly grave, his eyes came back to my face. I have no doubt that it was pale, and I am certain that it was solemn. "What the dickens is the matter?" he asked.

There was the sizzle of a siphon. Galliphant was mixing a drink at the sideboard. He came forward, and held it out to Voysey, who took it almost obediently, and drank.

"Thanks," he said, putting down the half-empty glass on a table at his elbow. Then he looked from one to the other of us again. "What has happened?" he asked impatiently. "What is wrong?" And he sat forward, impatience changing to alarm in his frank eyes.

Galliphant sank into a chair, fumbling for his cigarette-case. I pushed the box across to him, and he helped himself.

"My dear Frank," and his voice was now so calm and matter-of-fact that it sounded perfectly ordinary, "there is no doubt we have afforded Martin a very curious insight into the mysteries of hypnotism, although I am afraid that, so far, your performance continues a mystery to him, while it is of little value as a demonstration of the power of the hypnotizer's will over the senses and physical functions of the hypnotee."

"Indeed?" said Voysey, and seeing that a silence threatened to follow: "Tell me more about it," he begged.

"Another time," answered Galliphant, striking a match, and what time he paused to apply it to his cigarette, Voysey expressed his surprise at being thus put off.

"I want you," said Galliphant, taking no heed of Voysey's mild protests, "before we leave you to-night, to turn your mind to a matter that is no doubt as painful to you as it is to us all—for we all three loved Colin Chester. I want to ask you some questions regarding the circumstances that attended his death. You were at Cheynesworth at the time."

"Roger!" I cried, while Voysey looked from him to me, startled by my exclamation where he had only been surprised by Galliphant's calm words. The conclusion had forced itself upon me that Galliphant accounted Voysey in some way responsible for Colin's death, and that taking advantage of what Voysey had said in his trance, he was now for questioning him in a manner that struck me as being hideously unfair. If Galliphant must question him, at least, in common honesty, he must first inform him of what words he had uttered while unconscious. I was about to say so, when Galliphant's uplifted hand and impressive glance arrested the words on my lips.

"Wait Martin," he said, almost with a touch of sternness. "You don't understand. I can guess what is in your mind. But surely—surely you can trust me."

I grew instantly ashamed of the suspicion I had entertained, and I cast it from me, assured that Galliphant was not the man to take an unfair advantage of any one, much less of a friend. Not knowing what to think of this extraordinary situation, I sat still and waited.

"What is all this mystery?" inquired Voysey, as well he might. "It seems to me you fellows might take me into your confidence. It's perfectly plain to me that something odd has taken place."

"You shall be told everything in due time," answered Galliphant. "If I were to tell you now it might bias your answers to the questions I want to ask you. I would prefer that you answer them without knowing what prompts them. Do you mind?"

"Why, no," answered Voysey, between frankness and mystification. "But what questions can you possibly want to ask me about poor Colin's death? The whole matter was made clear at the inquest. I don't think I can add anything to the circumstances then made public."

"I rather think you can," said Galliphant in a voice that made me—knowing what I did—run cold, and awoke again momentarily my suspicions of his motives.

"The circumstances on which I require information may hardly be deemed connected with his death, and yet I have come to the conclusion that they may be. This conclusion may be idle and unwarranted; but I think you are the man to clear that up."

"I?" ejaculated Voysey. Galliphant disregarded the ejaculation.

"Colin died," he said slowly, "of a fall from a wall on the summit of which he was wandering in somnambulism. Can you recall any other case of somnambulism during your visit to Cheynesworth?"

Voysey was plainly startled by the question. He flushed slightly.

"Why, yes," he said, and it was clear that he spoke as much under the dominant influence of Galliphant's gaze as out of any inclination to do so, "I was a victim of it myself."

"That is what I had supposed," said Galliphant quietly. "But somnambulists are unaware of their affliction unless they happen to be awakened while walking in their sleep. Now, how did you come to discover that you were a somnambulist?"

"I awoke one night," said Voysey slowly; rather sadly, I thought, "to find myself at Colin's bedside; in fact, I awoke to find myself struggling with Colin. I had an Oriental dagger in my hand—a toy that he used as a paper-knife, and there were a couple of gashes in his pillow, where, it seems, I had stabbed it. It appears that Colin couldn't sleep that night, and he had the light turned on and was reading when I entered his room. That," added Voysey in a voice almost of horror, "was how he saved himself. The shock of it made me ill for a couple of days. I had a touch of fever, and"—he hesitated a moment, then went on—"and, as a matter of fact, I never felt quite comfortable in poor Colin's company, although he was most decent about the whole affair."

"Of course he would be," said Galliphant. "He could be nothing else. You would not have been likely to attack him in any other condition."

"Indeed, I would not, and I only hope he realized it fully. Our situation, you know, was peculiar. I mean with regard to Miss Cornaby. Most of the people at Marleford saw through it that he was entering the race against me, and some hint of it may have reached his ears afterward."

"Yes, yes," murmured Galliphant, soothingly.

"I can only imagine that a matter which I put from my waking mind must have preyed upon it sleeping, inspiring me with an unconscious enmity, and urging me to a revenge which my normal self had no thought of."

"Don't worry yourself with that," Galliphant interrupted. "Tell me now: How soon afterward was it that Colin died?"

"A week to the day."

"I see. Can you recall any circumstances at all out of the ordinary, any indisposition or appearance of indisposition on Colin's part, anything, in fact, that was not quite as usual on the day of his death or a day or two before it?"

Voysey pondered, mechanically stroking his fair mustache; Galliphant smoked in silence; and I listened and watched, a strange flutter pervading me, excited by a matter I did not attempt to understand. All that was clear to me was that Galliphant had drawn some definite conclusion from Voysey's words during his trance, and that his questions were set with some very definite end in view. But what that end was I could not attempt to guess.

"No," said Voysey at last. Then, suddenly recollecting: "At least," he added, "I remember nothing beyond the circumstance that Colin complained of a headache in the afternoon. But that is hardly of consequence, is it?"

"I can't say until you tell me more about it."

"I remember that we were playing tennis in the afternoon—several of us, among whom was Colin. He had to abandon the game on account of his headache. It came on rather suddenly, and it was feared that he had got a touch of the sun."

"Well?" inquired Galliphant. "Did the headache persist?"

"No!" exclaimed Voysey, and he almost shouted the word as a man will do under a sudden shock of memory. "I remember now. He was dreadfully concerned about it because the Cornabys and some other people were coming to dinner that night, and he was afraid he wouldn't be fit to receive them. But James Chester gave him something or other when he went up to dress, and to our agreeable surprise when he came down again he was as fit as ever I have seen him, all trace of the headache vanished. I remember that he——"

"How to you know that James Chester gave him something?" Galliphant interrupted. "Did he say so?"

Voysey took his chin in his hand, and was thoughtful for a moment. "I can't say how I know," he answered at length. "That is the impression that I have."

"But you can't recollect hearing Colin utter words to the effect that he had been cured by something his cousin had given him?"

"Well, no," said Voysey, mystification deepening in his eyes. "I don't remember that."

"Probably you and the others took it for granted—*supposed* it to be the case?"

"Very likely."

"I want you to try to remember what cause you had to suppose it; people don't arrive at conclusions without some sort of evidence."

"At this distance of time, I am afraid I really can't recollect that," said Voysey. "But, Look here, Roger, what are you driving at, anyway? I've been most patient, and——"

"Wait a moment like a good fellow. And do try to answer my questions to the best of your ability. There is more in it than you may think. Now let me try to help your memory. Were you perhaps led to suppose that James had given Colin some specific or other because, say, James accompanied him to his room when he went up to dress?"

"That's it!" cried Voysey. "That's it! My room was next to Colin's. I went up immediately after them, and as I reached my room Colin's door was closing, and I heard James' voice."

Galliphant sat forward, his face tense, his long, nervous hands clenched on his knees. Never in all the years of our acquaintance had I seen him so excited.

"Do you remember what he said? Do you remember what he said, man?"

"Yes," said Voysey. "He was asking Colin to let him see if he couldn't do something for his headache. That is how I gathered the impression, and, no doubt, I told the others when Colin came down cured, that James had found something to put him right."

"I see," said Galliphant, slowly, and he sank back into the depths of his chair, his eyes veiled behind half-lowered lids. "I see." He sat very quiet for a few moments, while neither of us spoke, realizing almost by intuition that his mind was wrestling with some elusive problem. At last he looked up again.

"I am sorry to trouble you further," he said, "but would you mind giving me once more the details of Colin's death, exactly as you witnessed it?"

"If you wish it. He was walking along the summit of the wall——"

"No, no," Galliphant interrupted. "Begin earlier than that. You were—several of you were—I believe, in the card-room, when Colin complained of drowsiness. It was midnight, and all the guests, with the exception of the men staying in the house, had left. I am right so far, am I not?"

"Yes," Voysey assented, and took up the tale. "James suggested to him that perhaps he had better be getting to bed, reminding him that he had been rather off color earlier in the day. He said 'good night,' apologized for leaving us, and went."

"Alone?"

"Quite alone.  We sat down to a last rubber, Robert taking his brother's place at our table. We finished it, and sat on, chatting idly, while at the adjoining table yet another rubber was in progress. The hall clock chimed one, and James got up, saying that he would turn in. I was of the same mind, and so we happened to leave the room together. Fred Massey and Robert went over to the other table to watch the end of the rubber that was being played there. James kept me talking in the hall, I remember; first about the clock, and then about antiques in general. We may have been there five minutes or so; then we went up-stairs.

"The rest you know. We paused on the landing by the old mullioned windows. There was a full moon that night; it was hot, and one of the windows stood open. I leaned out for a breath of air, and it was at that moment that I saw a man on top of the wall in his pajamas, walking with a firm, unfaltering step along that giddy height. I checked myself from crying out, realizing suddenly what was the matter, and how fatal it must be to wake him. So long as he slept he might be safe.

James at my elbow caught sight of him, too. 'Colin!' he whispered in a voice of horror, and at that moment the somnambulist faltered in his step, stopped, swung round, and with a cry pitched headlong over and outward into the park."

"You needn't trouble about the rest," said Galliphant, and again he lapsed into thought.

"It's an amazing thing," he said presently, "that nothing of all this should have come out at the inquest."

"But they are such trifling matters——" Voysey began.

"Trifling?" cried Galliphant, almost fiercely. Then he laughed savagely and rose. "They are so little trifling that they make all the difference between murder and accidental death."

"Galliphant!" we cried together. "What on earth do you mean?"

"Mean?" he echoed, his keen eyes darting from one to the other of us, and reflecting some of his scorn of our obtuseness. "I mean that Colin Chester was murdered, and that it shall be the task of my life to bring his murderer to justice."

### III.

When Voysey and I had recovered from the shock of amazement produced by that extraordinary statement of Galliphant's—an amazement that in my own mind was fraught with a momentary doubt of his sanity—our questions rained hot and fast. We reminded him again of the actual facts of Colin's death, and when he mocked us with the answer that it was precisely from those facts that he drew his awful conclusions, we demanded to be made aware of the stages of his reasoning, to be told upon what theories he based his tremendous supposition.

"It is no supposition," he answered us. "It is a certainty based upon facts that are perfectly clear to me, and upon conclusions that are as perfectly logical." And that was as much as he would say just then.

More we could not elicit from him, and when we attempted to insist, we provoked him into some expression of regret that he should have said so much. He assured us that we might spare ourselves our insistence. In the fulness of time, he promised us, we should know all. To tell us now, he added, might be to hamper such operations as he should decide upon. Not that he did not trust us. He trusted us implicitly. But the time for disclosures was not yet.

Our further persistent questions proved all in vain, and in the end, with the excuse that it was very late and time we were all in bed, he said "good night" to Voysey, and insisted upon taking me away with him.

Half-way down Regent Street we found a hansom, and apparently forgetting that I had my quarters in Ryder Street, he gave the driver his own address in Lincombe Gardens. In the cab he explained his reason, and I confessed that it gratified me with the promise it contained of dispelling my mystification.

"You are not going to leave me just yet, Martin," he said. "You and I must have a talk."

"Do you mean on the score of this affair of Colin?" I inquired.

"Yes," he answered. "I'll tell you when we get to my place. Meantime, let me think it out again." He leaned back in the hansom, smoking in silence, and in silence I sat beside him while conjecture after conjecture, each wilder than its predecessor, chased one another across my confused mind. I was at the highest pitch

of expectancy by the time we reached his compact
bachelor establishment. He was well-housed, with
comfort and with taste, and his study—into which he
now ushered me—was of all studies that I have ever
known the one that seemed pervaded by a true air of
studious seclusion and scholarly refinement; nor can
I picture any room that would have been in better
harmony with the man. It gathered dignity from the
somber rigidity of the choice Jacobean pieces with
which it was furnished. The thick, dull-tinted Eastern
rugs that left bare little more than a suggestion of the
polished floor beneath, and three or four low, ample
armchairs in dark-brown leather tempered with the
promise of comfort the rather severe elegance of the
apartment. The contents of the gleaming bookcases that
furnished the four walls gave a hint of the wide reading
of their owner.

On a sideboard stood decanters and siphons and a
little pile of sandwiches, besides cups, and a Turkish
coffee-pan on a small spirit-stove. Galliphant was
considerate to those in his service, as indeed he was
to all the world, and he never kept his man up if he
expected to be late.

He disposed me in a chair, then busied himself with
the spirit-lamp.

"You'll find the cigarettes beside you," he said, "and
I am going to brew you the strongest coffee you have
ever tasted. It is a wonderful quickener of the faculties
and I want yours to be at their quickest for what I have
to tell you."

"Before you proceed to do so," I said—for it seemed
odd to find him as ready to talk to me alone as he had
been unwilling to talk while we were with Voysey—"I

should like you to tell me whether in any way you suspect Voysey of being connected with Colin's death."

He shook his head, and smiled gravely. "No," he answered definitely. "I am absolutely sure that Frank had nothing to do with it. But it would not have been considered so extraordinary if he had; for you will remember that a motive could easily have been found for him; Colin had unwittingly robbed him of Miss Cornaby. I want you to keep that circumstance in mind. It was that coupled with the words he uttered to-night in his trance gave me the clue to the discovery of a crime of whose existence I had not dreamed."

"But why, then," I asked, "did you bring me here to tell me of your theories, whatever they may be, while you refused to let Voysey hear them?"

"You will understand that better just now. I may want you to come down to Cheynesworth with me. Had I revealed to Voysey what I am about to reveal to you, he would perhaps have insisted upon accompanying us, and not only would that have been inconvenient, but, possibly, painful."

He busied himself with his coffee-apparatus for some moments, during which I smoked and reflected. Presently the rich fragrance of his brew pervaded the room, and he served it—hot, black and frothy, a delicious beverage which I could easily credit with all the virtues of stimulation that he claimed for it.

"I will begin at the beginning," he said, as he sank into a chair opposite to me, "and if there is anything that is not clear to you interrupt me; but not otherwise."

I nodded, and he proceeded.

"Voysey's odd words in his trance to-night, coming at a moment when I told you that he would have no thought but my thought, no will but my will, were certainly very startling; they even seemed at first to prove me wrong and I confess that I was badly intrigued for a moment or so, until suddenly, remembering something that he had said, I realized what was taking place.

"There is such a thing, Martin, as the hypnotic memory. In hypnosis the subconscious mind alone is active, the subliminal self, if asserted, setting up between one hypnosis and another a well-defined relationship. In a hypnotic trance a man can have no recollection of anything that he may have said or done in his normal state and, similarly, in the normal state a man has no recollection of anything connected with his hypnosis. But just as memory in the normal mind links the happenings of one day to the happenings of another, so does the subconscious mind remember the transactions of a former subconscious state touching which the normal mind is blank. You follow me?"

"Perfectly," I answered, accepting his word for all this that he told me.

"Then you will realize that Voysey's subconscious mind was dwelling upon the happenings of a former hypnosis when you observed and were alarmed by the terrific distortion of his face. As soon as I had grasped that circumstance I set him questions to elicit what those happenings had been. You heard his answers, and you heard what further he had to tell us when he awoke. Between the event to which they referred and the death of Colin does no link suggest itself?"

"None that I can see," I answered, puzzled.

"Yet, if you will reflect, I am sure that you will see that a somnambulistic trance was the feature of both those happenings, and," he continued with singular impressiveness, "the object of both these somnambulistic trances was the same. They both aimed at the death of Colin. The first failed, because Colin awoke and, struggling with Voysey, awoke him also; the second, as you know, succeeded."

"My God!" I cried, still only half-understanding. "But these are mere theories, Galliphant."

"Theories? They are facts incontrovertible. Now follow me carefully. I shall approach the subject from another point of view. Assuming that Colin was murdered in proceeding to seek the murderer it is expedient to look round for a man with a motive. The first question to ask ourselves is: Who would be likely to profit by his death?"

"Robert Chester would succeed to the estates," I said.

"Yes," he agreed. "But Robert dies some four months afterward; it becomes almost a matter of discovering whether Robert also was not a victim. I am fairly satisfied in my own mind that he was. I shall return to that. Meanwhile let us look further for the man who is to make a profit."

"Are you in your senses, Galliphant?"

"If you will only wait, I will try to make the thing as hideously plain to you as it is to me. By Robert's death, following upon Colin's, James Chester is not only the gainer to the extent of the estates, but also to the extent of becoming engaged to the girl who was to have married Colin. This has more point than may at first appear; and I shall return to that also. Meanwhile let us pass on to assume James Chester guilty; it is a mere hypothesis at present; and let us return to a survey of the affair from its hypnotic aspect.

"When Voysey told us that he had attempted to murder Colin, he told us something that he had attempted to do in a former hypnosis, and, consequently, at the suggestion of the hypnotizer. You remember that hypnotizer's name, don't you? He mentioned it."

"James Chester!" I muttered stupidly.

"Yes, James Chester, and the assumption is therefore fairly justified that James Chester desired the death of Colin, that he sought to encompass it. In other words, we may look upon it as an attempt by James Chester to murder Colin. The attempt failed. But when a week later we find Colin walking to his death in a somnambulistic trance, it is reasonable to seek evidence of that trance having been induced just as Voysey's was induced. That is what I sought when I pressed Voysey with questions as to how he knew that Chester had 'given Colin something for his headache.' Shall I tell you what he gave him?"

"He hypnotized him," I cried, "to cure him by suggestion."

"Exactly; and he seized the opportunity—an opportunity for which you may be sure that he had been waiting—to impose certain commands upon Colin.

"'When you awaken,' I hear him saying, 'you will feel no headache; you will feel extremely well. But toward midnight you will experience drowsiness. You will go to bed and fall asleep. On the stroke of one o'clock you will rise, still in your sleep, and you will go up to the northern turret, and walk across the wall that connects it with the turret in the southern angle. When I call you, you will instantly awaken.'

"Having thus imposed his infernal commands upon Colin's subconscious mind, he would arouse him. The train was laid; the murder practically accomplished."

"But is all this possible?" I gasped, and then as suddenly I cried: "You have no evidence that Chester called him."

Galliphant smiled in a somber way. "It would now trouble me if I hadn't; but I have—of more than that. At one o'clock he rose, and Voysey rose with him to go up to bed. That, you will say, may have been coincidence. But was it coincidence made James dawdle in the hall and keep Voysey with him talking of antiques? To me it looks rather as if he were deliberately waiting to give Colin time to reach the wall, and keeping Voysey with him that he, too, might be a witness of Colin's end.

"Then they mount the stairs. They see Colin in the moonlight. Voysey hears James utter Colin's name in a voice of horror. But what he supposes to have been a horror-stricken ejaculation was nothing less than the call by which James awoke the somnambulist and hurled him to his death as certainly as if he had thrust him from the wall with his hands."

I was aghast, bewildered, and still incredulous. It seemed to me so unfair to attempt to establish an accusation by proofs so impalpable, so dark and so mysterious.

"After all, Galliphant, how can this be more than a theory?" I gasped.

"The attempted murder of Colin through Voysey is no theory. It is a fact of which we have testimony that admits of no doubt—the confession of Voysey's subconscious mind.

"Let us look more carefully into that attempt; let us analyze it, and see what it would have meant had it succeeded. It would have meant that Voysey would have been hanged for a murder in which he would most

certainly have been caught red-handed. He might have
set up the defense of somnambulism. But that defense
would have been deeply mistrusted, and it would have
been utterly damned by the fact that there was an
apparent motive for Voysey's taking the life of Colin.
Colin had supplanted him with Pauline Cornaby. Thus
at one blow James Chester would have rid himself of
a man who stood between him and the Cheynesworth
estates and of another who might come to stand between
him and the girl whom he desired—as we may assume
from the circumstance that he has since become
engaged to her. Do you realize now the fiendish subtlety
of the mind that chose Voysey for its instrument?"

"By Heaven! Yes," I cried.

"Well, then—realizing it, and having evidence that
James Chester hypnotized his cousin some few hours
before his death, can you still consider my theories
unproven? My dear Martin, I am as certain of what
I have stated as I am of my own existence. Give it
thought, Martin. Go over what I have said, and tell me
where you think my chain of evidence is weak."

I did so, and, as a result, conviction of the truth of
what he said sank into my mind, provided, of course,
that his scientific facts were right, and those I had no
reason to doubt.

Suddenly his passing reference to the possibility of
Robert Chester's having been another victim recurred to
me. I turned to him in agitation.

"But Robert Chester?" I cried. "By what means other
than natural can you account for his end?"

"Ah," he answered gravely, "there I grant you that
my reasoning relies more upon speculation than upon
evidence. But there is some evidence, too, of a kind.

His death puzzled the two medical men who made the post-mortem. Baffled, they put it down to heart-failure, as is so often the case. Yet it struck me at the time that the finding sounded rather absurd in relation to a young athlete of renowned endurance. But now that we know what James Chester accomplished in the case of Colin, a more reasonable explanation of Robert's end suggests itself. In fact, until he had disposed of Robert, he could reap no benefit whatever from his crime. Remember that James continued to live at Cheynesworth with its new owner. He had a way of winning confidence. In spite of his spendthrift, wastrel ways, his cousins were attached to him, particularly Robert. If we suppose that he found an opportunity to hypnotize Robert, the rest is easy."

"But how?" I asked.

"Perhaps I should not have said easy," he amended. "Certainly it would not have been quite as easy as in the case of Colin. True, James might have sent him along the wall at midnight, as he did his brother. But it is possible that he desired to vary his experiments. I can understand such a frame of mind. Now, it is well known that in hypnosis the operator can so weaken the pulsations of his subject as to cause the heart ultimately to cease beating altogether, leaving no lesion, no sign by which the diabolical violence exerted can be traced."

"Oh, it is horrible!" I burst out.

"Yes," he said, "and as probable as it is horrible."

"But are you sure that you are not taking too much for granted?"

"We have proved, I think, that James killed Colin, and if you will give the matter thought you will see that—as I have said—the work began by the destruction of Colin would not be completed until Robert also had been removed. Still," he concluded, "for lack of absolute proof, we are perhaps not justified in striving at any positive conclusion concerning Robert's death. On that score we will give James Chester the benefit of the doubt. But we must deal with him for the murder of Colin, since a singular chance, a strange fatality, has brought that crime to our knowledge."

"Deal with him?" I cried. "How can we possibly deal with him? You may convince me; you may make it as clear as daylight to the world with the arguments you have used and the testimony of what Voysey told us; but could you induce a jury to convict on impalpable evidence of this kind?"

"Of course not. That would be utterly impossible; and its impossibility was one of the first things I realized in connection with this hideous business. That is what I meant when I said that we should have to go down to Cheynesworth."

"Do you think that you can gather evidence that would be acceptable?"

He shook his head, his blue eyes troubled, his keen face somber to the point of sadness. "No," he said with a sigh. "That, too, would be impossible. I have all the evidence that I need, and it is all the evidence that there is. No more is to be obtained unless it be a confession from James Chester, and that is something too remote to be counted upon. No, Martin," he concluded, rising and speaking now with an impressiveness that was almost terrifying, "we are not going down to Cheynesworth to collect evidence. We are going down to administer justice."

I sat almost petrified, staring at his set face and great eyes that were turned full on mine.

"Do you hesitate, Martin?" he asked me. "There is no law that can touch James Chester. Is it not our duty, then, for the sake of the affection we bore the dead man, to take the law into our own hands and to avenge him?"

"But how?" I asked, and my voice almost startled me by its husky note. "If we—if we kill him, we expose ourselves to the justice he is evading."

Galliphant leaned toward me, and his eyes seemed illumined now by a light almost fanatical.

"Have no fear of that," he said, and a grim smile played round the corners of his stern mouth. "We shall fight—I shall fight him with his own weapons, and I, too, shall find a way to slay that will leave no lesion, no mark to betray my violence."

I do not know in what words I answered him, but when I left Lincombe Gardens in the gray light of that summer dawn I was pledged to join forces with Galliphant in the administration of a dark justice befitting the dark deed that called for it.

IV.

Deep and sincere had been Galliphant's friendship for Colin Chester, and thus his tremendous purpose of bringing James Chester to justice, of avenging upon him the subtle, diabolical crime upon the discovery of which we had so miraculously stumbled, will be readily understood.

Of the exactness of his conclusions not a shadow of doubt remained in me. However I may have reported his arguments in this narrative, to me they were of a lucidity, of a consequence that increased in a measure as I pondered them after I had left him. But when I attempted to speculate upon the methods he would adopt to discharge the avenger's task he had imposed upon himself, I found myself in a mental *impasse*. I could see no way in which, as he had sworn, he would combat and overcome James Chester by the very weapons that James Chester had employed to destroy Colin.

My confidence in Galliphant's powers was shaken during the hours of that night of agitated sleeplessness; from which you will see, when you come to learn the sequel, how much I under-estimated his subtlety, astuteness and resource. If I have—and rightly—qualified James Chester's crime as diabolical, I must confess that the same term would almost apply to the measures taken by Galliphant to avenge that crime—always, of course, with this difference, that in Galliphant's case the end no doubt was a justification of the means.

We left Paddington on the following afternoon, and went down to Marleford with our rods, ostensibly for a few days' fishing. There is a tolerable inn down there that places some two miles of preserved water in the Marle at its visitor's disposal, and at this inn Galliphant and I found comfortable quarters.

Galliphant was a passionate angler, and to see him at work upon the stream on the following day would have been to gather the impression that no care disturbed the serenity of his world, no purpose had a place in his mind beyond that of grassing trout. We fished upstream; the trout were rising well, and so much in earnest was Galliphant that his creel grew heavy as he went. Still, far from the object of his visit being forgotten in the fascination of the sport, that sport itself was but a part of his Machiavellian scheme, and when we came to the end of the hotel water he deliberately scrambled over a wall into Cheynesworth Park and without hesitation became a poacher. The inevitable fate of a poacher of such brazen methods overtook him before long. I was some four hundred yards below him on the opposite bank when we were hailed by a keeper, who was almost speechless with indignation.

"Hi! What are you doing there? Don't you know that this is private?"

Galliphant affected innocence. "I know," he said. "But, you see, I am staying at the Marleford Arms."

"Marleford Arms be damned," swore the keeper. "You're a mile beyond the hotel water. This is Cheynesworth Park." And with some further very forcible but entirely unnecessary criticisms, he proceeded to demand Galliphant's name and address. Roger expressed regret at a trespass of which he suggested that he had been unconscious, and gave the man his card.

"My friend on the other side," he added, "is of course within his rights."

"Within his rights?" gurgled the excited keeper, who was red in the face. "This is all Cheynesworth Park water—both banks." And with that he made his way across by a rustic bridge a few yards higher up, and came down to seek my name and address as well. Following Galliphant's example, I also gave him my card, and with that we departed to the sound of his terrific threats of legal proceedings.

The motive for all this was hardly clear to me at the time; perhaps I am not quick at inference; I certainly came to that conclusion that evening when, an hour or so before dinner, James Chester drove up to the door of the inn.

There is a pleasant lawn in front of the Marleford Arms, facing the river across the road, and out here Galliphant and I were seated enjoying the cool of the evening at the time. I had asked him one or two tentative questions as to his intentions, but he had put me off with a smile, bidding me wait.

At sight of us James Chester hurried forward, and at last I understood why Galliphant had led me to commit that trespass earlier in the day.

"My dear Galliphant! My dear Scholes!" exclaimed Chester, his manner genially excited. "What on earth do you mean coming down to Marleford without letting me know? I can't tell you how vexed I was when my keeper brought me your cards—vexed with you fellows for having permitted yourselves to be driven out of the park. Surely you know that the water is entirely at your disposal. Really, I take it as almost unfriendly that you didn't look me up as soon as you arrived."

He rambled on in this fashion, shaking hands with us, and remonstrating more and more with us on the score of our behavior. He was a giant of a man, not much over thirty, broad and immensely powerful of frame, with a huge head of crisp brown hair, and a round, red, clean-shaven face in which a pair of eyes, small, brown and beady, were deeply set.

Galliphant's manner was one of friendliness tempered with dignity. He assured him that we had arrived at Marleford only the day before, and that we certainly should not have left without running up to see him. We intended, Galliphant thought, to stay about a week or so. Chester pressingly invited us to put our bags in the dog-cart and become his guests at Cheynesworth. But considering our mission the idea of this was no doubt as repugnant to Galliphant as it was to me. We excused ourselves as best we could. We dwelt upon Chester's exceeding kindness; another time we should be delighted to avail ourselves of his hospitality; but for the present occasion of our sojourn at Marleford we would content ourselves with coming frequently to see him.

He stayed with us some little time; drank an *apéritif* with us; and when he departed, it was arranged that we should dine with him at Cheynesworth on the following night. He also pressed us to look up the Cornabys, assuring us that they would be delighted to see us, and this we promised to do next day. With that he left us; climbed into his dog-cart, and, taking the reins from his groom, whipped up and was gone. I experienced a sense of relief from the moral nausea that had been coming over me.

"He hardly has the air of a murderer," said Galliphant coolly, as we went in to dinner; and, indeed, nothing more remote from the criminal type could have been imagined than smug James Chester. He was the picture of content—a man pleased with himself and at peace with the world, a good-natured, easy-going, self-indulgent type of man, exceedingly commonplace.

So much was he all this, that Galliphant's reasoning, which had appeared so clear and lucid to me in town, seemed now fantastic. I found it almost impossible to associate so infernal and cunning a crime with so ordinary a man, and fresh doubts began to assail me.

The following afternoon found us, true to our promise to Chester, at Rose Cottage, the little hillside residence of Mrs. Cornaby and her daughter.

We had known them intimately in the old days, before Colin's death; and they received us like old friends. At least, Mrs. Cornaby did. Never had her manner been more gushing. Pauline was more reserved, with a reserve that impressed me rather oddly from the first.

Nor was that the only thing about her that impressed
me. In the old days, with her sunny hair, clear gray eyes,
good height and healthy complexion, she had been the
embodiment of all that is most admirable in the more
vigorous type of modern English girl. To-day she still
preserved her sunny hair and lissom height; but the
brightness was gone from her eyes; the elasticity had left
her figure; she moved listlessly, almost with the air of
an invalid, she who had been so brisk and so vigorously
erect. Her complexion was gone, and her cheeks were
pallid. She was thinner, too, altogether more fragile, as
if her health had suffered. And the moral transformation
in her was more remarkable, more pitiable than the
physical change. She had been as alert and active of
mind as of body; talkative in a bright and witty way;
a girl who struck one as being capable of thought
and feeling. Now, all this was gone; she had little
conversation, and what she had was dully couched and
uninteresting. In general, a more deplorable change it
would be difficult to conceive than that which had been
effected in Pauline Cornaby in the space of one little
year. Was it Coin's death, I wondered, had so affected
her; or could it be that her worldly, domineering mother
had compelled her into an engagement to James Chester
that was wholly distasteful, and that has so preyed upon
her mind as to have wrought this transformation?

I noticed that Galliphant, while he talked to Mrs.
Cornaby, kept his eyes turning almost continually to the
girl's face, as if he were studying it and scrutinizing it.
Her mother caught him at it in the end, and drew him
away to discuss, as he afterward told me, Pauline's state
of health with him. Galliphant, however, put her off. He
pleaded that as a doctor he was of no account, having
acquired little of the experience that is founded upon

active practise; but he could not refrain from adding that the change in Pauline was so marked as to call for attention—more marked, perhaps, to him who had not seen her for so long, than to her mother who had never been separated from her in the interval.

It was a scorching afternoon in the early part of July, and it can be particularly hot in the valley of the Marle. Tea was served on the lawn, in the shade of a couple of great cedars, and I continued to discuss trivial matters in a trivial manner with Pauline, while Mrs. Cornaby engaged Galliphant's attention with persistence.

Pauline strove, it was plain, to lend a polite attention to my words, and that obvious striving was becoming painful. It had been clear to me for some time that talk of what I would, her interest in what I said was simulated rather than real; but now as I chatted— striving gallantly to maintain the conversation under these very trying circumstances—she ceased to interject even the monosyllables with which hitherto she had been making a pretense of attention. Her manner became distrait; her air, I observed, was almost that of a person who is listening for something or some one she expects. Presently a little color crept into her cheeks, a sparkle to her eyes, and she seemed in an instant to have become once more the bright, desirable Pauline Cornaby I had known.

I was amazed by the suddenness and unaccountable nature of this change, which Galliphant, I noticed, had also observed. There was a look of inquiry, almost of astonishment in his glance as it turned aside again and again to scan her face. Then came the oddest thing of all. Quite suddenly she emitted a sharp cry, as of pain, and her hand flew to her ankle.

"Dear! What is the matter?" cried her mother.

Her flushed face gradually paled again to its normal hue. She smiled reassuringly. "It is nothing," she cried. "My ankle hurt me for a moment." Yet there was nothing to account for it; her foot had protruded from beneath her skirt a moment before, entirely at rest.

Galliphant's gaze was full upon her, more searching, more inquiring than ever. He was obviously puzzled.

And as he watched her, she rose abruptly, and took a step forward, expectancy in her face. An instant later James Chester came into view at the far end of the lawn, beyond the tennis-court, and I heard Galliphant catch his breath sharply. A clump of laurel had screened Chester's approach, and the turf had deadened—to me, at least—all sound of his steps. It occurred to me that Pauline's senses must be singularly acute.

She left us without a word, to run to meet him. Galliphant looked at me, and I thought there was an odd gravity about his face, a significance about his glance, which, however, I was utterly unable to read.

Then Mrs. Cornaby's slow, commonplace voice was uttering commonplace words; never in the whole course of her useless life do I think she ever uttered anything that was otherwise.

"The dear child is so fond of James," she was informing us. "Fate works so mysteriously. I often think it was for this that Colin was taken," was her preposterous statement.

"I have no doubt it was," answered Galliphant, with a daring grimness that would have been unwise had the words been addressed to a person of keener perceptions.

Chester approached us briskly across the lawn, Pauline clinging to his arm, her face upturned to his. They made a picture that some might consider loverlike; to me it was singularly repellent, for there was something about Pauline's air and look that was anything but pleasant.

Chester was the very essence of filial devotion to Mrs. Cornaby, the very essence of boisterous, breezy cordiality to us.

We remained at Rose Cottage for perhaps an hour after his arrival, for our visit, after all, was hardly one of ceremony; and when, at last, we took our leave, Chester rose, too, to accompany us. It had been arranged that we should dine with him that night, and he offered this as his reason for going so soon.

At parting Mrs. Cornaby invested us with the freedom of Rose Cottage for as long as we might remain at Marleford, and upon that we shook hands, and left.

There was a rather pretentious drive leading up to the cottage, closed by double gates, with a stile at the side for pedestrians. Galliphant who was in front had his foot on this, when Chester called out to him to be careful.

"The top plank is loose," he said. Galliphant got over carefully, then turned, smiling, to Chester.

"I hope," said he, "you didn't make the discovery for yourself."

"I did," answered James. "I meant to tell Mrs. Cornaby about it; but I forgot. It is positively dangerous."

"Has it been like that long?" asked Galliphant. We were all in the road by now.

"Not to my knowledge. I only made the discovery this afternoon, and it nearly cost me a sprained foot."

Galliphant laughed, and answered with a platitude. "We have to pay for experience, Chester," he said, and we went on down the dusty road talking of trivial matters until we reached our inn two or three minutes later. It stood at little more than a stone's throw from the gates of Rose Cottage.

Here we parted with Chester, and no sooner were Galliphant and I in our room than I inquired into his impressions of Pauline.

"What do you make of the girl?" was my question. He took off his tweed hat, and leisurely wiped his brow, but excitement glimmered in his eyes.

"What do *you* make of her?" he asked, in a tense voice.

"I?" I faltered, unpleasantly impressed by his manner. "I can make nothing of her; she puzzles me. At first I set down this change in her to Colin's death. I imagined that her scheming mother was forcing her into a distasteful marriage with James Chester. But when James appeared——I broke off as a fresh idea occurred to me. "By Heaven!" I cried, "did you notice that she seemed aware of his presence before we saw him?" And some dim notion of what was in Galliphant's thoughts leaped suddenly into mine.

"I did," said Galliphant. "I noticed *everything*—the doglike manner in which she fawned on him, in which her eyes followed his every movement. "Oh!" he cried, "it is awful! It fills me with disgust."

"You mean," I said slowly, "that she is another of James Chester's victims?"

"The girl that you saw to-day," he answered me, "had of the old Pauline little more than the body; the outward form. Her soul, her mind—call it by any name you like—is in bondage to that villain. You did not believe in hypnotism a week ago, Martin. You are likely to become more than convinced of its terrible potentialities before you leave Marleford.

"I have studied all the phenomena connected with it; but there are few, after all, that I have ever had an opportunity of actually observing. I knew of the existence of the phenomenon of *rapport*, and I have read of the wonderful mental and physical connection it sets up between hypnotizer and hypnotee. But not until to-day had I beheld a case of it. You know what I mean by *rapport*?"

I nodded. "But how could he have gained such an ascendency?" I asked.

"He has gained it," said Galliphant, "and that, after all, is what matters. I have no doubt he gained it before he attempted to make love to her. Had he begun by showing his intentions toward her, she would have mistrusted him, and he would never have had his opportunity.

"I am afraid we have been rather hard on that girl, and Voysey's judgment was a little rash. Certainly we have done her an injustice, but who could have dreamed of such a state of things as this?"

"Who, indeed?" I groaned.

"I imagine James Chester insinuating himself—with Mrs. Cornaby's delighted approval—into Pauline's friendship by his hellish sympathy with her in her grief at Colin's death. Now, grief has a way of weakening, of blunting the faculties. I have no doubt that Chester found some opportunity of giving her 'something for one of her headaches,' just as he gave poor Colin 'something.' His experiment succeeded, and made her the readier to beg a repetition of it, since it procured her ease; no doubt there were many repetitions, and with each her mind became more and more enslaved to his until there came a day when her will-power was utterly demolished, and she was his creature to be used by him as best should suit him. She dwells in a perpetual state of semihypnosis."

"Surely," I cried out, my mind revolting against accepting a thing so monstrous, "surely this is the merest speculation!"

"Oh, no," he answered, sadly and impressively. "It is a study of cause based upon the close observation of effect. The conditions we have seen to-day in Pauline Cornaby could not have been produced by any other means. If she has a headache now, I believe that he could cure it though he were fifty miles away, by simply willing her to feel it no more. She is aware of his presence before her senses could inform her of it, as you saw to-day, and before such a pitch of communication as that can be established things must have gone far indeed. I wonder did you see as much as I saw?" he asked suddenly. And then, without waiting for my answer, "Did you notice the incident of the stile?" he inquired.

"The incident of the stile?" I echoed, at a loss.

"Evidently it had no significance for you, Martin, yet it was that as much as anything else that brought me to my conclusions."

"Tell me," I begged him.

"I was about to question Chester as to whether he had hurt his foot this afternoon, when suddenly he volunteered the information himself by warning me of the stile; in answer to the subsequent seemingly casual questions you heard me ask him, I elicited that it had almost cost him a sprained foot an hour before. You noticed that just before he appeared Pauline cried out, and carried her hand to her ankle, telling us that she had felt a sudden pain there."

"God in heaven!" I ejaculated, and I sat still under the shock of realization that had burst upon me. "Can *rapport* account for that?"

"I know of nothing else in the world that can. It was plain to us all that she had in no way hurt her ankle. What she felt was a reflection of the pain James Chester was experiencing at that very moment in the corresponding part of his own foot."

It sounded plausible, but not obvious; and I still resisted conviction; resisted it although my every instinct seemed to assure me that the thing was so indeed. Perhaps I grew alarmed lest I should be lending too ready a credulity to the things that Galliphant was stating, to the theories he set up and labeled facts. I grew afraid lest carried away by a settled conviction we should be finding reasons, however monstrous, that fitted into that conviction. I said all this to Galliphant, seeking to check and warn him. But in his mind there was no doubt to be awakened. I even spoke of Mrs. Cornaby.

"How could such a state of things be possible," I asked, "without her mother observing the signs of it?"

"Mrs. Cornaby is singularly lacking in observation," he answered.

"Perhaps. But however lacking, she could not, surely, be blind to a condition so marked."

"I allow that it is extraordinary. But remember that Mrs. Cornaby is an exceedingly foolish woman, whose desire to see her daughter mistress of Cheynesworth Towers very evidently outruns every other consideration. If I do not say that she is unscrupulous, it is because a mind like hers is not to be judged by ordinary canons."

I was silent a while considering what he had said; then I returned to my expostulations.

"You shall be fully satisfied that I am not wrong," he promised me. "I will prove my statements; prove them beyond the faintest shadow of doubt; and I will do so to-night at Cheynesworth. But," he added, "I implore you to be careful that you are not betrayed into surprise, or into any expression that might suggest to Chester that you observe the strange things that may occur."

I confess that that dinner-party was the most unpleasant one of my life. I was acting a part. I felt myself a bloodhound in human guise, wearing dress clothes and dining at the table of the man upon whose trail I had been loosed. The sensation was not pleasant, and it was by an effort, by a series of efforts, that I contrived to keep a normal countenance and take my share in the conversation.

Besides the Cornabys and ourselves there was only one other guest, a young man named Fletcher, an acquaintance and neighbor of Chester's, a person of no consequence whatever in this story; probably—to judge by externals—of no consequence in any story.

We played a foursome at billiards after dinner; Galliphant and I against Chester and Pauline. Fletcher discoursed platitudes to Mrs. Cornaby, who reclined somnolently on the divan.

Pauline played a good game; in fact, a rather extraordinary game for a girl; but then she had always been good at games. Galliphant told me afterward that he believed Chester's mental influence directed her play—a circumstance that brought "Trilby" back to my mind with unpleasant force. But that is by the way. I had been instructed by Galliphant in certain experiments that I was to conduct for my own satisfaction, since I entertained some doubt of his statement of the *rapport* existing between Chester and Pauline. Finding a suitable opportunity I dropped the butt of my cue sharply on Chester's toes in the act of tendering him my cigarette-case. I was in line with Pauline, who was standing by the scoring-board at the far end of the room. Chester had his back to her at that moment.

He emitted a yell at the blow—it seems he suffered from a troublesome corn—and he took a couple of hops on his sound foot, with the one I had damaged held at the height of his knee. I was profuse in my apologies, eloquent in censure of my clumsiness. Galliphant and Fletcher laughed; Galliphant to mark his unconcern; Fletcher because he was a fool. But over the hopping Chester's shoulder I saw while apologizing a spasm of pain ruffle Pauline's face, and I observed that she held one foot from the ground.

I was rudely shaken by this fresh piece of evidence, yet I was not quite convinced, which shows to what an extent I had set myself to resist conviction. I contended that it must be remembered she had been a witness, and that a sensitive, affectionate woman in the intensity of her concern for the person that was hurt under her eyes, might by a quite ordinary reflex action be affected as she was affected, though perhaps scarcely to the same extent. Still, as I came to think of it, the test was hardly entirely satisfactory to me. The second one, however, was culminating indeed.

Chester detested whisky. The very smell of it nauseated him. We were aware of this, and we made use of our knowledge to apply the second test. An array of decanters, siphons and glasses stood on a silver tray on

a table in the window-bay. Chester had poured himself
a Benedictine, and had drunk half of it. He was in play
when Galliphant sauntered across to the table, and
poured into a liqueur-glass exactly the same quantity of
whisky as Chester had left Benedictine in his. He made
a pretense of sipping it. Then he set his glass down on
the tray, beside Chester's, and turned to face the others.
In that moment I called across the room. Very naturally
he turned again, picked up his glass, and came. But the
glass he now brought was Chester's not his own.

He stood chatting with Mrs. Cornaby, Fletcher and
me for a moment, his elbow touching the mantelpiece.
In the most natural manner he set his glass upon it,
when Chester, having broken down over an easy shot,
reminded him that it was his turn to play.

Chester moved down the room toward the tray, and
I went with him, forewarned of what was prepared. No
circumstances could have been more favorable for the
experiment. He stood with his back squarely turned
to Pauline, and there was, besides, the length of the
room between them. She was at the far end of the table,
leaning on her cue, watching Galliphant's series of
caroms. The steadiness of his nerves at that moment was
a thing that amazed me to the point of awe—and the
man an inveterate cigarette-smoker and coffee-drinker!

I stood beside Chester, but facing the opposite way,
looking down the room, so that by a lift of my eyes I
could watch Pauline. At Chester I had no need to look.
I knew exactly what would take place. He lifted the
liqueur-glass, and must have tossed off the contents
at a gulp, without giving himself time to perceive the
aroma. There was a splutter at my side and a nauseated
"A—h!"

Across the room, at the same moment, Pauline shuddered, and her face was screwed for a second as the face of one who had swallowed an unpleasant drug.

"I say," gasped Chester, wheeling round. "Who on earth has been putting whisky into my glass?"

Galliphant missed a losing hazard and looked up. "Whisky?" he said. "I say, have you been drinking mine?" He crossed to the mantelpiece to verify the circumstance.

"Yours?" cried Chester. "Do you mean that you drink whisky as a liqueur? Odd taste, isn't it?"

"Mr. Galliphant is an odd person altogether," purred Mrs. Cornaby, and there the matter ended.

But at our inn, late that night, Galliphant asked me was I satisfied.

"I am satisfied," I answered him, and I could not repress a shudder of repugnance at the thought of that girl's enslavement, "and I think we have come very opportunely."

"You are right, Martin," he said. "We imagined that the task set us by Fate would lie in punishing a murder. But it looks as if we were intended to do more; to prevent an even more dreadful crime—the slaying of a soul."

"The task will not be easy, Galliphant."

"I only hope that it may not be impossible. "Anyway, we act to-morrow night if things go well."

"To-morrow?" I was startled by the imminence of an action I could only contemplate with some equanimity while it was remote.

"Yes," he answered. "I have made arrangements. Chester has a wonderful collection of china. I manifested such an interest in china this evening that he asked me to go up and have a look at it quietly to-morrow night, when there will be nobody else there. Of course you are to come with me."

We certainly went to bed on that; but I as certainly never closed my eyes in sleep until the sun was streaming through my windows.

### V.

I slept late as a consequence of the insomnia that had visited the earlier hours of my lying in bed, and when I went below the clock in the bar was striking ten.

I made my way to the little room in which we had our indoor being, rang for breakfast, and picking up what letters there were for me, I moved across to the window to inhale a breath of that glorious summer morning. I was just in time to see Galliphant's tall, active figure come swinging down the road with creel and rod.

From his general air and the cheerful "good morning" he gave me, one would scarcely have imagined his mind oppressed by any weight of impending horrors. He raised the lid of his creel for me, and bade me wait for breakfast until its contents were made ready.

His manner chilled me. That one could yield up his mind to thoughts of angling with such a business as was ours on hand was something far from my own troubled understanding. I felt almost a dislike for him in that moment. But once we were alone, he threw off his careless demeanor like the cloak it was, and throughout breakfast, when it came, he was silent and absorbed, eating but little.

I have had occasion to allude before to the resource and subtlety of Galliphant's mind; and surely never was such a call made upon his resource and subtlety as that made by the manipulation of the events of those dreadful days at Marleford. And it was all done to the end that James Chester should be completely off his guard and without the faintest suspicion of our purpose. This was perforce essential to his plans, as you will realize presently. It was with this end in view that he had neglected to look up James on his arrival, preferring that James should learn from his water-bailiff and through the cards demanded from us, of our presence at Marleford. In submitting his belief in the *rapport* established between Chester and Pauline to tests that should place it beyond all doubt, he had acted with the greatest care and circumspection. And with the same subtlety had he paved the way to our forthcoming fateful visit to Cheynesworth.

He had—although I was in ignorance of it at the time—brought a book on china with him from town, and he had been cramming hard in the last couple of days a subject of which hitherto he had possessed only the most superficial knowledge.

A collector's weak spot is invariably his collection, no matter what that may consist of. Of all forms of vanity that crave for flattery and attention there is none so hopeless as the collector's, none that insists upon so much indulgence. He will waste hours and days upon a man whose society in general ways would be entirely uncongenial to him, if only that man displays an interest in his collection and some knowledge of its subject.

Galliphant's show of interest in Chester's china, accompanied by the scraps of recently acquired knowledge he had let fall, had been sufficient to cause Chester to insist upon our second visit; and—what was more important—that he might be free from interruption, or indifferent listeners to the lecture he no doubt proposed to deliver upon the subject of his hobby, he would take care that nobody else should join us. Indeed, I am sure that it was only by an enormous concession to the demands of courtesy that I was invited to accompany Galliphant.

I scarcely know how I got through that day. Galliphant fished. He was in the habit of saying that it was the finest mental rest he knew, inasmuch as it reduced his mind to an absolute blank. That may be why he had recourse to it on what otherwise must have been the most nerve-racking day of his life. It certainly was of mine.

Evening fell at last, and through the gathering dusk we strolled up to Cheynesworth. Through the gloom of the park we made our way, approaching the Towers on the eastern side. We emerged into a clearing, and paused almost at the very spot where Colin met his death. Actuated no doubt by the same thought, we stood there a moment gazing up at that precipitous wall from which our poor friend had been hurled by the infernal power of his cousin's will.

In the old days, no doubt, that wall had been embattled, and a parapet would have run immediately beneath and behind it, establishing a communication between the ancient turrets that still stood at either extremity. But of the original Cheynesworth that had been fortified against the Parliament in the days of Charles the Martyr there remained little now but the outer walls. The interior had been almost entirely rebuilt at different times. And in the course of one of these reconstructions the merlons had been swept from that wall, leaving it smooth as we now beheld it. The parapet probably vanished at the same time, and it can only have been from reasons of sentiment that the wall was not brought down to the level of the roof, which sloped behind it and some way below its summit. It had been allowed to remain, however, gaunt and precipitous in its enormous height, a relic of the former castellated appearance of the sixteenth-century home of the Chesters.

We went round to the main entrance, and the couple of hours that ensued were taken up with the ostensible purpose of our visit—the inspection of Chester's collection, and the attention to the lecture he delivered us concerning it. In these matters I have just enough taste to satisfy my own purposes, and I am neither a dilettante nor an authority.

The collection viewed and expounded upon, *ad nauseam* so far as I was concerned, we passed into the room that James made peculiarly his own and termed, for purposes of expediency, his study. There we sat down to a pipe and a whisky-and-soda before separating, and with that the curtain was rung up upon the preliminaries of the awful and astonishing duel of which I was the only witness—a duel which it is my firm opinion has no counterpart in fact or fable.

Galliphant led up to it in the most natural manner conceivable. From china he guided the conversation on to the subject of prints; from prints he steered it easily to pictures, and from pictures to books. From literature to the drama it is but a step, and so we were presently discussing the modern theater in all its aspects.

It was Chester himself who was the first to mention "Trilby." There was nothing extraordinary in that; indeed it was unavoidable in any conversation relating to the stage, for it was still the most talked-of play in town.

Galliphant shrugged his shoulders at the mention of it, and attempted to dismiss it with an impatient allusion to its flagrant absurdities. Naturally enough this provoked from Chester the same expostulation that I had provoked, with a similar statement, from Galliphant himself a few nights before.

"What do you mean by its absurdities?" he asked; and shifting his great bulk, he threw one of his massive legs over a second chair.

"I mean all the hypnotic rot that forms the basis of it. I can quite understand that it should be popular. The occult always is popular, and always will be as long as there are charlatans to practise it."

Chester moved his leg from the second chair and sat up, looking at Galliphant in some astonishment. It is not to be supposed that a man can make a study of hypnotism and carry out the experiments that Chester had been guilty of without having the subject very near his heart. Next to china—if not, indeed, before it—there was none other so engrossing to him, none that he would have been so eager to defend from such aspersions as Galliphant had seemed to cast upon it. And Galliphant had counted upon this when he so aspersed it. The attention it claimed from Chester proved how accurately Galliphant had gaged his depths. It was, I thought, yet another instance of the delicacy of Galliphant's methods.

"What do you mean by that?" cried Chester indignantly, and his deep voice sounded almost like a growl.

Galliphant laughed. "Hang it all," he exclaimed, "you don't mean to say that I am outraging any settled convictions of yours, do you?"

"I have an idea," said Chester between banter and seriousness, "that you don't know what you are talking about."

Galliphant took a quiet pull at his cigarette. "You are like a good many other people, Chester. You imagine ignorance of a subject to be the portion of every man whose views of it do not happen to be coincident with your own. Now, as a matter of fact, Chester, I have read a good deal on hypnotism in my time, just as I have read a good deal on a good many other subjects."

"That's it," said Chester, with clumsy playfulness, "you have read too much ever to have read one thing thoroughly. Beside, you're a doctor, and your studies of the material have prejudiced you where the immaterial is concerned."

"My dear fellow," said Galliphant, "I will repay you the compliment I had from you just now. You don't know what you are talking about. Hypnotism has been studied to some purpose by men of my profession, and if it is not employed more for clinical purposes, it is because its limitations have been recognized as not allowing for it."

Chester exploded at that. He got heavily to his feet, and inveighed against the whole tribe of medical men, dubbing them a parcel of quacks who lived like journalists, by the art of effectively concealing their ignorance. Galliphant, on his side, keeping his temper and even displaying a shade of tolerant amusement, which obviously served the purpose of driving Chester to exasperation, retorted with all the arguments that are used by the ill-informed in their denunciation of mesmerism in all its branches. There were moments when I almost heard myself speaking again—in the fullness of my ignorance—I had spoken that night at Voysey's apartment.

"I can believe in the sleep induced by tiring the eyes by a protracted stare at some bright object or other; but I can believe in no more, because that is the entire sum total of hypnotic phenomena."

"You think so, do you?" growled Chester. "I should like to show you how wrong you are." And he positively leered at him.

"You would have your hands full, I can assure you," answered Galliphant.

"What would convince you?" Chester asked him suddenly.

"Nothing," Galliphant retorted with finality. "Come, now, my dear fellow," he proceeded, in a humoring, coaxing tone, "you don't mean to say that you attach any importance to such clap-trap."

Chester turned from him impatiently. "What is your opinion of all this, Scholes?" he asked me.

"I know very little about it," I answered him. "Fight it out with Galliphant. You'll find him more than a match for you. He's as obstinate as a mule."

"My methods of convincing are fairly direct," said Chester. And he deliberately challenged Galliphant to submit himself to a test of the Lloyd Tuckey method of fascination by the eyes.

"I didn't know you were a hypnotist," said Galliphant, in the tone of one making light of another's powers. "Heavens! Martin, it seems I have brought my coals to Newcastle with a vengeance."

"You may laugh as much as you like," Chester retorted sourly, "but if you'll submit to me, I'll change your laughter."

Still they argued; Galliphant ridiculing, and Chester, exasperated by this ridicule, urging him to submit to the test of the power he sneered at.

For a moment I imagined that Galliphant's plans had miscarried for once. In his subtleties he had overreached himself, and I could not for the life of me see how he was to gain his ends by the road along with Chester now appeared to be urging him. The greater, then, was my astonishment when presently he rose, dropped his cigarette into an ash-tray, and pronounced himself entirely at Chester's disposal, defying Chester to convince him of the truth of the theory of fascination.

I glanced at James in that moment. Galliphant had his shoulder to him, in the act of draining his glass of very weak whisky-and-soda, and the look in Chester's eyes was so purposeful and malicious that I went cold with apprehension. In that moment I almost fancied that he had seen through Galliphant's purpose, whatever it might be; that he had somehow stumbled upon the suspicion that Galliphant had discovered the secret if not of Colin's death, at least of Pauline Cornaby's "possession." The subsequent events, however, proved how wide of the mark were my conclusions, and drove me to seek elsewhere an explanation of that light of triumph that had gleamed a moment in Chester's beady eyes. It was Galliphant who, later on, threw a plausible light upon the subject for me. Hypnotism and the craving to hypnotize may have become something of a mania with Chester. The successes that we knew he had achieved— and Heaven alone knows what other victims may have fallen to him—had emboldened him. He had tested the singular power of those hidden forces he could exert, and it may well be that he missed no opportunity of adding fresh subjects to the fell dominion of his will. From the reflection that here was another human soul that would presently become his slave, may have sprung the evil satisfaction that gleamed for a moment in his eyes.

"Where shall I sit?" asked Galliphant innocently.

"Oh, anywhere," growled Chester between boastfulness and carelessness, so confident was he of his power, so satisfied of Galliphant's utter nescience. That answer, and the frame of mind that dictated it gave Galliphant an unexpected advantage. He dropped— heedlessly, it appeared—into the nearest chair. But it was more than mere coincidence that he should be facing the light, while Chester's eyes must perforce be in shadow when he pulled up a chair and planted himself squarely opposite his subject.

I moved my position to their flank, whence I could watch them both, an odd excitement pervading me at an arrangement which left me plunged in speculative wonder.

"I will only ask," said Chester, "in common fairness that you do not attempt to resist me. Not that it really makes much difference, so long as you keep your eyes on mine; but the experiment would take longer; the result would be delayed."

"I understand," said Galliphant evasively, and with that they engaged.

At last I began to have something more than a suspicion of the singular duel that was taking place—all unconsciously on Chester's part. Never did second in any fight with material weapons experience greater concern for his principal than did I now as I watched them.

They sat erect, their hands upon their knees, like a couple of figures in an Egyptian fresco, beady brown eyes intent upon large keen blue ones. And they contrasted oddly; the one massive and powerful, his rugged plethoric face somberly set under crisp brown curls; the other slender and lithe, his clear-cut, almost ascetic countenance impassive and gathering dignity from its crown of thick white hair.

Thus they sat for some minutes without sign from either to show in whose favor the victory was inclining. Galliphant's was the face I mainly watched in my anxiety for him. A full five minutes may have sped when I saw his eyes grow suddenly a shade wider open than they had been. A panic seized me. As they dilated, the stare of those eyes appeared to grow more fixed. I looked at Chester, and my heart seemed now to be thumping in my throat; his lids were flickering, and they drooped slightly, as if a heaviness oppressed him. But even as I looked he seemed to throw off the threatened somnolence, and his glance resumed its deadly stare. I looked again at the other. Their breathing and the ticking of the clock on the mantelpiece were the only sounds that disturbed the stillness of the room where that gigantic struggle was being held. Galliphant afterward told me that the ticking of that clock was a disturbing factor, and but for that the struggle would have been less protracted.

Suddenly, as I watched him, Galliphant's lips parted.

"You are going to sleep, Chester," he said in a voice scarcely louder than a whisper. But its intonation made it more than a mere comment. Subdued as it was it had the confident note of a statement of fact. "You are going to sleep," he repeated, and I realized now that he was adding suggestion to fascination.

Chester's eyelids were closed, and as Galliphant repeated his words, a deep quivering sigh fluttered from his lips. Galliphant's voice, sounding like the drone of some great insect, again broke the stillness.

"Go to sleep," it said. "Go to sleep, Chester. Go to sleep—to sleep—sleep."

And as if in obedience to that dominant murmur, Chester's breathing grew heavy and regular, his figure rigid, and a line of moisture gleamed on his brow, which seemed to have gone pale for once. Galliphant was leaning forward, and making slow downward passes within a few inches of Chester's face.

A spasm of horror brought me to my feet.

"Roger!" I exclaimed in a voice subdued by awe.

He turned toward me, rose and advanced a step or two in my direction.

"Yes?" he inquired, entirely misunderstanding my exclamation. "What is it? Speak up; you need have no fear of awakening him. The battle is won, and he will never awaken now until I bid him. The trance is too deep."

"We can't—we can't do it," I stammered. "It is too ghastly—too damned cowardly."

He pushed back the white hair from his brow with a gesture that was almost of weariness. I have no doubt that the strain upon him in the last few moments had been enormous—for it had been a double strain of resistance as well as compulsion. Then he swung his arm to point to the decanters.

"Better have a drink," he suggested. "It will steady you."

I obeyed him, and when I turned to him again, I found him pulling steadily at a cigarette. My eyes shunned the bulky figure stiffly upright in its chair, as instinctively as they would have shunned the sight of a dead body. To my mind there existed too much connection between the two. Then a fear suggested itself.

"What if any of the servants should come?"

"I don't think any will unless we ring. Anyhow, we should hear them crossing the library, and the obvious thing to tell them is their master has had a fit."

I was overwrought and almost feverish with excitement, and an odd sort of fear.

"Galliphant," I besought him, "wake him up, and let us go. We are usurping the justice that is God's. We have no right to do this thing. Leave the avenging of the murder to——"

"And what of preventing that other and greater crime?" he asked with a singular and reproving dignity that made me feel as if my expostulations had been cowardly and childish. "What of that? Is this monster to be left free to pursue his career, ruining souls as well as bodies?"

"Is there no other way? Is there nothing you can do to break his power?"

"So far as Pauline Cornaby is concerned there is nothing any one can do to break it at this stage; not even he himself. His death alone—or at least, years of separation—can release her from so profound a thralldom."

I stood wringing my hands like an imbecile, utterly unnerved; and yet I know that I am not a coward. With weapons or without them I would have encountered Chester any day, and sought by physical means to exact justice from him. But to take justice from that limp, helpless, defenseless mass!

I said as much. Galliphant smiled with a sad tolerance. I seemed to react upon him in such a way that the more excited I became the calmer did he grow.

"What of the fight I have fought?" he asked. "He is helpless now, you say. But if you had conquered him with carnal weapons would he not lie just as helpless? My dear Martin, I have met him and defeated him with his own weapons. I knew no more than that such a thing was possible, that there are cases on record where the hypnotizer employing the method of fascination has, himself, become hypnotized. And depending upon that I pitted my strength against his, and I have conquered. Was I cowardly? Has not this murderer had more than fair play already? Come, you are weak, and false scruples are blunting your judgment. I have laid him low; the rest is as necessary as the burial of the dead. Look upon it as nothing more."

"What do you propose to do with him?" I asked hoarsely, still far from convinced.

He was silent a moment, his face very grave and even pale, but his eyes firm and determined. "He must die either the death of Robert or the death of Colin," he said in a low voice. "There must be an end of him; as much to avenge the things he has done as to prevent the worse things he may yet do."

I shrank from him, and sank limply onto a couch. My elbows on my knees, I covered my face with my hands, partly because I was overcome with horror; partly to shut out the sight of that stiff, heavily breathing figure.

"Martin, Martin!" Galliphant expostulated. "Think of Colin; think of Robert; think of Pauline, and think, too, of Voysey. This is not a time for ordinary measures. Had I not trusted to your strength, I should not have brought you with me."

"Give him a chance, Roger," I implored, looking up, "a chance that will make this look less like murder."

He took a turn in the room, his chin sunk forward on his breast, his brows knit in thought. He paused again in front of me.

"Very well," he said. "He shall have that chance. You shall not say that I killed him in his sleep, as he killed Colin. I shall impose my will upon him, and then wake him, and tell him what we have done. Will that satisfy you?"

"Where is the difference?" I cried. "It is not giving him a chance, it is simply informing him that you have dealt him a mortal blow. But the blow itself will have been struck while he is helpless."

"Yet it will rest with me whether it shall prove mortal or not. If he prefers the justice of the law-courts, he shall have it. Provided that he supplies me with a written confession I will stay my hand when the time comes."

The difference may after all have been slight, but it made the concession to my feelings for which I craved that I might know some peace hereafter when this thing was done. I nodded my acquiescence and Galliphant turned from me, and went across to Chester's side, while I sat and listened to the commands he imposed upon the sleeper. They were worded almost identically with Galliphant's reconstruction of the suggestions by which Chester had sent Colin to his death.

"It is now a quarter to twelve," he said. "After you are awake, and in a quarter of an hour's time from now you will feel drowsy; do you understand?"

"Yes," came in a whisper from Chester's parted lips.

"You will go to bed and to sleep. But on the stroke of one o'clock, being still asleep, you will rise from your bed, and you will make your way to the northern turret. You will climb through the window onto the wall, and you will walk across it to the southern turret, into which you will also climb by the window. But should I call you at any moment during that time, you will instantly awaken. Do you understand?"

"Yes," came Chester's voice again.

Galliphant stepped back, and his arms dropped heavily to his sides, a gesture that eloquently suggested how overwrought was his mind. Then he braced himself to the completion of his task.

"Wake up, Chester," he commanded, and his hands played rapidly above the entranced man's face.

Then he surprised me by taking up the comedy of being hypnotized exactly where it had been interrupted. He dropped back into his chair opposite Chester as the latter opened his eyes. Galliphant's face was set and purposeful as is the face of a man going into battle.

Chester heaved a deep sigh, and his eyelids rolled back slowly. He stared before him in utter silence for a moment or two, his face expressionless. Slowly life and animation crept back into it. He emitted a grunt, and shifted in his chair; then he uttered a faint laugh that suggested confusion, and in that moment Galliphant spoke in a voice that was cold and incisive.

"You don't seem to have made much of a success of your experiment, Chester. Am I to sit here all night?"

"Eh?" said Chester, and no doubt he now imagined that he had dozed off for no more than a couple of seconds. "I am afraid I am not equal to the strain to-night. I have had a long day in the fresh air. To tell you the truth, I am feeling rather tired."

"You will feel still more so in a quarter of an hour's time," said Galliphant, and he rose.

"Eh? Why?" asked Chester, rubbing his eyes, and sitting forward.

"I have hypnotized you," Galliphant informed him.

He was on his feet in an instant, white as death. He had good reason from his own experiences with others to dread such a performance upon himself.

"You've done what?" he bellowed.

"It seems I couldn't help it," answered Galliphant, coolly and very much as ease. "You opposed yourself to a mental vigor greater than your own, my friend, and you fell a victim of it. In seeking to fascinate me, you became, yourself, fascinated. That is all."

Now, there was nothing in this to justify the storm of fury that broke from Chester and betrayed him. Oaths and vileness of speech poured from his lips in an almost incoherent torrent, revealing the blackguard that lurked behind the thin veneer of his ordinary civility. Galliphant's cold voice, his eyes, looking almost terrible as they fastened upon and held the other's glance, arrested him.

"Why all this excitement?" he asked. "I have done no more than you proposed to do to me. And if I was ready to consent to being hypnotized by you, why should you fly into a passion because our little experiment has resulted in the reversing of our positions?"

Chester's mouth fell open and his eyes rolled stupidly for a moment, showing that he felt the force of Galliphant's logic. Then the fear that was in him mastered his common sense.

"It's a trick," he snarled. "You told me a damned lie when you said you knew nothing about hypnotism. You've done it on purpose to get the better of me."

"I never actually said that I knew nothing about hypnotism," said Galliphant. "But in what way do you suggest I might have got the better of you?" And again his words fell upon Chester's fury like cold water upon hot metal; and seeing that he got no answered, Galliphant proceeded:

"Or is it that you fear that I shall use the power I have acquired over you as you used yours over Colin and Robert and Pauline Cornaby?"

That was a bludgeon-stroke indeed. Never have I seen a change more awful come so suddenly over mortal man. Chester staggered back as if he had received a crushing blow; he even put up his hands half-way, as if to avert another. His face turned ashen; his eyes bulged hideously in his great face, and suddenly his knees were loosened, and with a gasp he sank back into the chair from which he had lately risen. Vainly did he seek to control himself: The bluster was all quenched in him like a fire that is stamped underfoot.

"Are you mad?" he asked in a hoarse voice.

"Not in the least."

"What are you saying, then?"

"I am giving you a chance which you never gave either Colin or Robert. I am forewarning you. Thus you can put right your affairs and make your peace with God. For as you dealt with them, so have I dealt with you."

"You are mad," he persisted, his guilt written in the vile scrawl of terror across his bloated face. "You are mad."

"I came to Cheynesworth to do this thing," Galliphant went on, "and I have done it. I have doomed you to walk along that wall by which Colin went to his death, and as Colin awoke at your call, so shall you awaken at mine, unless——" He paused intentionally.

"Unless?" cried Chester. He was so utterly stricken as to have forgotten to keep up a pretense of innocence.

"Unless you choose another road. Unless here, now, at that desk, you write a full confession of your crimes, which I shall carry away with me to hand over to the proper authorities. Make your choice, Chester. Will you pay the penalty at my hands, or will you take your chance of the law?"

Then, at last, Chester recovered. "I think it is *you* that will have to deal with the law," he sneered. He sat forward in his chair, resting his elbow on his knee, and looking steadily at Galliphant. "Let me understand more clearly what you threaten," he said. "You talk of things of which I know absolutely nothing. But if you have played any tricks of suggestion with me—by God, I'll make you smart for it!"

Galliphant eyed him sternly. "Don't you think it will save time if you drop this pretense of not understanding me? You must imagine me to be very blind if you think I could have avoided perceiving the nature of your influence over Miss Cornaby. Moreover, it is a matter which I could have little trouble in proving by evidence and test."

"No doubt," said Chester ironically, now more master of himself. "And no doubt you would prove with the same ease your charges concerning Colin—whatever they may be? Meanwhile, I should like you to be a little more explicit regarding them."

Briefly—with a brevity almost contemptuous—Galliphant recited for him the more salient features of his crime as he had reconstructed it from what Voysey had told him. And he startled Chester, too, by alluding to his victimizing of Voysey. He must have been sorely puzzled to discern how Galliphant had come by such unerring and particular knowledge.

"And you think," said Chester with an undercurrent of defiance, "that from such materials you could make out a case that would be convincing to a jury?"

"I don't," answered Galliphant, "and it is because I don't that I have fooled you into giving me an opportunity of hypnotizing you."

"That's a lie. You never hypnotized me."

"Indeed I did, as Martin can assure you."

Chester scowled at me, but asked no questions. He got heavily to his feet once more, his face empurpling, and his eyes so wicked that I thought he was about to fling himself upon Galliphant. Indeed his next words showed that that had for a moment been his intention. His glance shifted again from Galliphant to me. I, too, was on my feet now.

"You damned cowards!" he snarled at us. "You are wise to come in pairs to insult me."

"Martin has not said a word yet," said Galliphant scornfully. "He is here to see fair play."

Sneeringly Chester looked again from one to the other of us.

"And you think to get the better of me?" he asked.

"I think," said Galliphant, "that I have already accomplished that. You are in my power—just as Colin was in yours. And unless you prefer to write out that confession you shall walk the wall to-night."

"To-night!" echoed Chester, and again his courage seemed to desert him. His face paled and twitched. "To-night!" he repeated, staring wildly. Then he steadied himself, and walked deliberately across to his desk.

"You shall have your confession," he muttered. A sigh of relief broke from Galliphant. Chester pulled open two drawers, one after the other, and rummaged for a moment in the second one.

It certainly seems to me now that from our knowledge of the man we should have mistrusted that sudden acquiescence. But we stood there idly watching him, mildly surprised, until suddenly he turned with a sinister laugh, and we saw that he had possessed himself of a pistol.

"You shall have your confession," he repeated, "since you insist upon it." His manner was now fiendishly mocking. "I did kill that fool Colin, and that other fool his brother. How you came by your knowledge I won't pretend to guess; but it may be of some satisfaction to you to know that you are as much in possession of the facts as if you had witnessed the deeds. I tell you this," he went on, his tone bitter and sneering beyond description, "because in the pass to which things have come the knowledge will be of little use to you. I die neither by your contriving, nor by the law; but here and by this, and you Galliphant, go with me for your infernal meddling."

And with that he slowly raised his arm, bringing his pistol into line with Galliphant's head. I moved forward with a cry of alarm.

"Stand back there," he bade me, leveling the revolver now at me, "or I'll put a bullet through you first."

Instinctively I came to a standstill, and in that instant Galliphant spoke. He was very pale, but he held himself erect, and his voice was never calmer.

"One moment, Chester," he said. "Are there no terms you might care to make with me?"

"Terms?" said Chester, in surprise. And then he laughed contemptuously. "You're afraid, are you?"

Galliphant shrugged his shoulders and spread his hands in an eloquent gesture. "Why not?" he said. "It is the only reasonable frame of mind in my present position. Besides, it is usual to offer terms of surrender before proceeding to bombardment."

Chester considered a moment. Then he slowly shook his head. "There can be no talk of terms between you and me."

"Wait a moment," Galliphant again besought him.

"Wait? Wait for what? For one of the servants to come to your rescue, I suppose. That is what is in your mind." And he laughed at his own acumen. "Are you ready, Galliphant?"

"No, I am not. Lock the door if you think I am trying to gain time hoping for one of your servants to interrupt us. Only do let us talk this thing over."

It was as plain to me as no doubt it was to Chester that to gain time was Galliphant's only aim. I wondered did he hope for some help from me, and was it to give me an opportunity of aiding him that he was seeking to prolong this parley. Realizing my impotence to help him I was driven to despair; a despair quickened by the reflection that it was I and my scruples had placed Galliphant in this position. How bitterly then did I not reproach myself for my weakness in urging him to give

Chester a chance. This was what had come of it. It was likely to cost Galliphant his life.

"There is no more to be said," Chester answered him, but without sneering now. Instead, his voice had the ring of a deadly resolution, and his face was set, his glance baleful.

He leveled his pistol again, and a grayness came over Galliphant's face as he stared at the nozzle. A sickness seized me. For a moment the room seemed to rock. Yet Chester did not fire. I steadied myself, and looked at him. And then an amazing thing took place—amazing, at least, to me. Chester's eyes assumed a dreamy, far-away expression. In the hall the clock was striking twelve; the little clock on the overmantel took it up at that moment. Gradually Chester's arm, uplifted to fire, sank back to his side. A slight tremor seemed to run through him, and a prodigious yawn threw wide his jaws.

Then in a perfectly ordinary voice, as if resuming the thread of an interrupted leave-taking: "You must really forgive me for turning you out like this," he said. "But I'm not equal to it. I've had a long day." He yawned again, and looked a moment at the pistol in his hand. "Useful thing," he said foolishly, and returned it to its drawer. "I don't believe I ever felt so sleepy in my life. Suppose it's liver. Well, good night, you men."

At last I understood. He had come under the influence of Galliphant's post-hypnotic suggestion. It was for that that Galliphant had been seeking to gain time. With a gasp of ineffable relief I turned to Galliphant. The grayness had left his face, but he preserved his calm. He took my arm, and in silence we turned and left the room, Chester following to see us out, yawning as he came, and mumbling excuses in a drowsy voice.

But he forgot to perform the duty of escorting us to the door, for as we were passing the stairs he seemed to grow unconscious of our existence. Obeying the commands imposed upon him while in his trance, he turned aside, and without another word to us, proceeded to make his will-less way to bed.

We let ourselves out, and drew the hall-door after us.

## VI.

Slowly, silently and thoughtfully we made our way through the park. It was a perfect night. The moon rode at her full in a cloudless sky, almost directly overhead, flooding the valley with her white light.

Not until we were out of the Cheynesworth domain did Galliphant break the silence.

"I have been through the valley of the shadow to-night, Martin," he said. "But I am glad, for it has served the purpose of drawing a confession from him, and we have now his own word for it that we are justified in carrying out the thing that brought us here."

It was so, indeed; and even I who had hitherto held back and who had jeopardized Galliphant's life that night through my aversion to the blow's being struck, was now satisfied that at all costs Chester must be removed. Self-defense rendered it as imperative almost as justice—particularly for Galliphant.

But in Galliphant's tone I detected a fresh note. He spoke like a man who is wedded to a task of whose lawfulness he has need to assure himself lest the resolution to carry it through should fail him. And surely a man who had been so firm and relentless before had no cause for weakness or relenting now. Yet it almost seemed as if the experience he had undergone that night had sapped his nerve and undermined his courage. And of this I had presently abundant proof.

We were half-way perhaps between the gates of Cheynesworth and our inn, when he suddenly came to a standstill in the middle of the road.

"I can't do it," he burst out without warning. "Martin, I thought I could; but I can't! I can't!"

To my mind, however, he had done it already. What more was to come was inevitable. So I took his arm, and seeing how utterly his calm had deserted him, I sought to soothe him.

"It's all right, Roger," I said, combating his repugnance. "Never let it disturb your conscience, particularly now that we have Chester's own assurance of what he has done. It is necessary for Pauline Cornaby's sake."

"If it were necessary for my own sake I couldn't do it now. Martin, a thing like this must be done quickly. Too much brooding over it unnerves a man. I thought I was strong enough and brave enough to stand the strain. But—my God! —I'm not."

"How can you prevent it now?" I asked.

"I could call upon Chester to awaken now. The distance is nothing. If I were to do so, it would release him from my influence. Or," he continued, "I could fail to awake him now or at any time to-night, and he would walk that wall in comparative safety in his sleep."

"And in that case," I asked, "what would become of Pauline Cornaby?"

We seemed to have changed places in the last few minutes. In a measure as he weakened in his purpose, I seemed to gather strength and my heart hardened against that brute who would have added the crime of shooting us to the many others his soul was already charged with.

"Ah, yes," he muttered, "there is Pauline." Then turning to me: "There might be another way so far as she is concerned. I could find a couple of medical men to come to Marleford and observe her and the obvious power which Chester has acquired over her. He might be brought to account for that."

"He *might*," I said dubiously. "But do you really think he would be? And if he were, how would that help her? You have said, yourself, that nothing short of his death could liberate her from his thrall. Besides," I cried, "after what we saw to-night of what he can become at bay, do you really think he would be an easy man to bring to book? Galliphant, your own life isn't safe now, while he's at large."

"I can take care of myself," he answered. "My own danger mustn't be weighed in this balance. Don't you see that that is just the consideration that does most to arrest me? As long as my frame of mind could be utterly impersonal, I held myself justified. Now all that is changed."

"Roger," I answered, "you are starting at shadows. You have gone too far to draw back. It would be dangerous and foolish."

"But, Martin," he exclaimed, "is it really you who are urging me to go through with this thing? You, who less than an hour ago were imploring me to abandon it altogether! I wish I had listened to you then."

"Much has happened since," I replied. "Until then there was no actually direct evidence of Chester's guilt. Now we have his own confession."

He returned to me no answer, and we went on a little way. Then he stopped again. In the distance, at the foot of the hill, gleamed a light, revealing the position of our inn. A little way beyond it and up the hillside to the right I saw another light, which I apprehended in a subconscious sort of way to be shining from one of the windows of Rose Cottage.

"I think, Martin," he said, and his voice had resumed much of its habitual calm, "that I will let matters remain just as they are, leaving the rest to the will of Heaven."

"What do you mean?"

"I will do no more than I have done. Neither will I undo anything. Chester shall walk that wall, and whether he crosses it in safety or stumbles and meets his death, shall be as Fate decrees. I will not awaken him. I have brought him to the block, Martin; but I can't summon courage to raise the ax."

I took his arm, and we went on in silence. In a sense I think this resolve was, to me also, the most satisfactory. If Chester should chance to fall in the course of his perilous nocturnal walk, we should be spared the feeling that we had pushed him over.

Galliphant peered at his watch in the half-obscurity. "Come," he said. "It is half-past twelve already." And we stepped out more briskly, reaching our inn a moment or two later. But on the matter of going to bed, we hesitated. Galliphant led the way into our little room, and turned up the lamp. I followed, and crossing to the window I threw it open, and leaned out.

Galliphant came over to me, dragging a chair with him. "We'll wait," he said, and sat down beside me by the open window. I was perched on the sill, gazing out at the stars; Galliphant smoked; and throughout the ensuing half-hour or so I don't think we exchanged four words. Our nerves were all on edge.

At last, vibrating like a note of doom, the hour of one boomed out from Marleford Church. It was echoed almost immediately by the stable clock at Cheynesworth; then all was still again. Galliphant had risen and was standing beside me breathing heavily in the excitement that had come upon him. It was an excitement that instantly infected me; my temples throbbed and my hands shook in the grip of it.

We said no word, but I am certain that our thoughts ran a parallel course. They were with the man at Cheynesworth. Now he would be rising from his bed. The minutes sped swiftly. Now he would be making his way down the long corridors of Cheynesworth Towers; now climbing the stairs that led up to the turret from which he was to emerge. A wild hope surged in my mind that he might find the door locked and the key missing; which only serves to show how ill-balanced was my mind that night, that I could blow hot one moment and cold the next. And now he would have opened the door, and crossed the threshold of the little turret-chamber. He would be going forward toward the oriel opening that was windowless as that of a belfry. I glanced over my shoulder at the clock. It was seven or eight minutes past one. Yes; he would have got that far by now.

Abruptly my thoughts were diverted. With a quick indrawing of breath, Galliphant, too, had leaned forward in that instant. A sound of running feet pattered on the still night air, accompanied by a panting that was almost like the sound of sobs. Something white dashed across our line of vision, speeding up the road that ran beyond our little lawn.

"It's a woman," Galliphant exclaimed in a whisper. "It is——" I heard no more. He had gone through the window, and was crossing the lawn at a run. I went after him, and rejoined him beyond the garden-fence. Ahead of us, speeding up the road at a rate almost incredible, went a woman in a white evening-gown. As by one accord we started to follow.

"It must be Pauline," he cried as we ran, and from the odd significance of his tone, I grasped the unspoken notion that had flashed into his mind. We had forgotten all about the extraordinary *rapport* that existed between Chester and his latest victim. Yet what we beheld was no doubt the work of it. That sympathy of thought must have warned her now in some subtle way of his deadly peril, and obeying some impulse that it would be idle to seek to explain, she was hastening to him.

She headed straight for Cheynesworth, and just beyond the park gates we made a desperate effort to overtake her. Galliphant had himself well under control again by now, and he was thinking hard, already anticipating for the girl a dreadful danger of whose existence I did not so much as dream.

Her speed was something phenomenal, and Galliphant in spite of the fact that he was wiry and athletic, could not, exert himself as he would, outstrip her. As for me, I had already fallen behind. We swept round a bend of the avenue, dashed down a side-path, into which Pauline led the way with unwavering certainty.

Surely, surely Chester must be either dead or safe by now, I thought. He had had more than time to cross the wall, assuming that my calculations of his progress had been exact.

Out of the dark lane through a clump of firs I dashed, into the clearing on the eastern side. I came to a halt at the very spot where Galliphant and I had paused that evening on our way to call on Chester.

It was the thing I beheld brought me to that standstill, utterly unnerved. Along the summit of the wall at a height of some fifty feet, a figure looking black in the moonlight was moving slowly. It was a good three-quarters of the way across, and it was advancing steadily toward the southern turret. And then, before I had time so much as to wonder whether he would reach it, a piercing scream broke upon the stillness of the night. It was Pauline, whom Galliphant had failed to seize in time.

"Jim! Jim!" she cried out twice, and the figure on that fearful causeway halted abruptly in its calm progress, then crashed down without a sound, and lay in a heap at the foot of the wall.

It had been left for Pauline to become Colin's and her own avenger.

As Chester fell I caught the sound of a moan, the most awful I think that I have ever heard from man or beast, and Pauline lay unconscious in Galliphant's arms.

He turned toward me, and in the white light of the moon his face looked ghastly. "This is indeed God's justice," he said in a thick voice. "You had better call assistance," he added more calmly. "And be careful of what you say. Tell the exact truth, omitting only the circumstances of Chester's trance. Make haste, Martin."

I went on my errand. I hammered on the great doors of the hall, and I was answered sooner than I expected. Jeans, the butler, accompanied by one of the footmen, confronted me half-dressed. They had been roused by a woman's scream, they said; and they were full of questions as to what had happened.

"Your master is probably dead," I answered. "He was walking across the great wall, presumably under exactly the same circumstances as poor Mr. Colin."

Jeans, who had long been in the family, had a very vivid recollection of that earlier tragedy. He followed me with shaking knees, and behind him came the scared and gaping footman. Between them they carried all that was left of James Chester into the hall, where a crowd of frightened servants had gathered by now. Galliphant brought up the rear with me, and between us we bore the unconscious Pauline.

In his capacity as a doctor, Roger made an examination of Chester, and to his surprise found him still breathing. Galliphant assumed command of the situation, and ordered one of the footmen off to fetch a carriage from the stables—the first he could get ready. While waiting for it, he gave Jeans his orders.

"I am going to rouse Doctor Morton," he said. "Meanwhile get somebody to help you carry your master up to bed. But carry him with great care, and don't attempt to undress him until the doctor comes."

The footman returned presently with a half-dressed groom, bringing a park phaeton. It was hardly the most suitable kind of vehicle, but as they explained, it was the only one they could get ready quickly, as they hadn't the keys of the coach-house where the other conveyances were kept. We lifted Pauline onto the back seat, and Galliphant got up beside her.

"You had better drive, Martin," he said. "Stop at Doctor Morton's. Here, what's your name"—this to the groom—"you had better come with us; never mind your clothes. We shall want you."

The man obeyed him. I took the reins, and three minutes later we were at Doctor Morton's door. Galliphant had given the groom his orders as we came along. The fellow jumped out as I drew up.

"Straight on—to Rose Cottage," Galliphant bade me, and I whipped up again. As we reached the gate of Rose Cottage we met Mrs. Cornaby and her maid. They were alarmed, and in search of Pauline.

We carried the girl into the house, and laid her on a couch in the morning-room. She showed no signs of reviving from that frightful swoon. I wanted to ask questions, but Galliphant gave me no time.

"Now back to Morton's," he ordered me. "The doctor should be ready by the time you get there. Come back to me after you have taken him up to the Towers."

"Is there any hope for James Chester?" I asked at last. It was a question I had been wanting to ask for some time.

"None," he answered definitely. "It was his back."

I went out, and drove back to Morton's, and pondering what Galliphant had said. A terrible judgment had overtaken Chester. He had perished by the hand of his own victim. There was in this something so overwhelmingly just and fitting as to make it indeed look like the justice of Heaven that Galliphant had proclaimed it. The recoil of his wickedness it was that had slain Chester—and I was singularly relieved and comforted by that reflection.

I found Morton waiting. He was at his gate when I dashed up, listening to the groom's excited story. He jumped in, and we raced back to Cheynesworth at a gallop.

He made his examination, and looked very grave.

"Shall we undress him, sir?" asked Jeans. "His man is here."

The doctor shook his head. "It is not worth while— just yet," he said. "A flicker of life may remain for some hours yet, but he will never recover consciousness. There is nothing that I can do."

He turned to me to ask me for particulars of the tragedy. I told him how we had seen Chester walking along the summit of the eastern wall, obviously in his sleep.

"Strange," he muttered very seriously. "He is the second Chester to meet his death that way. I should pull the wall down if I were the heir." Then with a sudden lifting of the eyes, he asked me the obvious question; the question I had been expecting: "How did you happen to be on the spot at the time?"

I told him that we had been with Chester until midnight, and that returning to our inn we had been sitting at the open window, smoking a pipe before turning in, when we saw a woman race past us up the road. Imagining that we recognized Miss Cornaby, and thinking something must be wrong we had followed her. But she had run so fast that we found it impossible to overtake her until she had brought us to the scene of the tragedy almost at the very moment at which Chester fell. Indeed, but for her cry it was possible that Chester might have been more fortunate than Colin, for he was almost across at the time.

Morton nodded, and peered at me through his gold-rimmed spectacles.

"All this is very strange, is it not?"

"Very," I answered laconically.

"And Miss Cornaby?" he inquired. I told him of her. "Come, then," he said. "You must drive me back there. I may be of use. Here I can do nothing."

As we drove away again he leaned toward me. "Mr. Scholes," he said, "although the man is almost dead I can't help saying that in to-night's happening I see the hand of Heaven."

"What do you mean?" I cried, not a little startled.

"I mean," he said very seriously, "that there was something I could not help observing in the course of my acquaintance with Mrs. and Miss Cornaby. Chester had obtained a wicked hold over that girl, and he has been punished. But for that he might—as you have suggested—have crossed the wall in safety."

So! The thing was so obvious that even this easy-going, commonplace country practitioner had noticed it. What, then, was Mrs. Cornaby doing? Her blindness must indeed be willful, as Galliphant had suggested.

We found the cottage all alight, and Galliphant met us in the hall.

"Glad to see you, Morton," he gravely greeted the doctor. "Miss Cornaby has partly recovered consciousness. But I almost think it would have been better if she had not done so until after."

"Until after what?" asked Morton.

"Until after Chester has gone. There is something I think you had better be told at once, doctor," he began. But Morton surprised him, as he had surprised me, by revealing what he had already learned from his own observations.

Galliphant and Morton watched at Pauline's bedside with Mrs. Cornaby throughout the greater part of that awful night. She lay moaning and complaining of excruciating pains in her back and legs, which any one less acquainted with the extraordinary circumstances of the case would have set down to delirium. Morton considered it extraordinary and, perhaps—in his heart of hearts—very interesting. Galliphant was appalled by it. He told me afterwards that he thought he must go mad that night, as he watched in her the reflection of such sensations as Chester must have experienced had he been conscious.

Toward five o'clock in the morning a great weakness seemed to oppress her, and her lamentations grew more and more enfeebled. Her voice was failing, and her pulse so extraordinarily weak that Galliphant's secret fear began to change to certainty that she would die with Chester.

A few moments later, however, her complainings ceased quite suddenly, and she sank into a gentle sleep.

Galliphant rose from his chair with a fervent "Thank God!" Morton looked up suddenly, and in some surprise.

"What is it?" he asked.

"Sh!" whispered Galliphant, and beckoned him from the room. Outside he showed the doctor his watch. It was a quarter past five. "James Chester has just died," he said, "and I was thanking God that Miss Cornaby had survived him."

At the inquest on James Chester the story Galliphant and I had to tell was identical with that which I had told Morton. The coroner pressed for some elucidation of the mysterious manner in which Miss Cornaby had been drawn to the scene of the tragedy. But Galliphant and Morton shrugged their shoulders, and spoke vaguely of telepathy.

With Miss Cornaby a profound sympathy was expressed; but I am inclined to think that it was superfluous.

She awoke to consciousness a few hours after sinking into that peaceful slumber for which Galliphant had rendered such devout thanks to Heaven, and when I saw her again a couple of days after the inquest, I found her once more very much as I had known her of old. The last few months had left upon her mind the impression that she had been very ill, and she was tormented now and then by elusive memories. But time mended that; time and Galliphant, for here again he took affairs into his masterful hands. Before we left Marleford he had a private interview with Mrs. Cornaby. I never had the details of it, but I know that he read her a severe and perhaps rather impertinent but certainly effective lecture on the duties of a mother, on the evils of selfishness and worldliness.

Striking while the iron was still hot, and acting before the effect of his words could entirely have worn off, he told Voysey the whole truth of the matter, and sent him down to Marleford as soon as we got back to town. The Cornabys came up to London three months later, and six months after that—Voysey and Pauline were, at last, very happily married.

# The Dream

## I.

### STANLEY BICKERSHAW

The colonnade is undoubtedly the most distinctive feature of Herne Place. You step from its broad shelter on to a pathway of red gravel, wide enough to admit a carriage, and beyond that there is a sweep of meadow, smooth and level as a lawn, flanked on either side by woodland, sloping gently to the river half a mile or more away.

Anthony Orpington had acquired that imposing residence on retiring from the Stock Exchange, and in the cool shade of the colonnade he was entertaining to tea, on a languorous afternoon in July, his nephew, the celebrated Stanley Bickershaw.

There was no point of family resemblance between the two men. Orpington, who was in his sixtieth year, was very tall and spare, with fine hands and an aristocratic, sallow face. He was dressed with care in a grey lounge suit, and he wore white spats—an inevitable part of his apparel— over his enamelled shoes. A soft grey hat covered his thinning hair, and a single glass in a tortoise-shell rim adorned, or assisted, his left eye.

Bickershaw was short and of a weedy, delicate build. His face was sallow, but with an unhealthy sallowness which in a man of his years—he was not more than thirty—argued sedentary habits. His nose was heavy and pendulous, his lower jaw remarkably heavy, his mouth little more than a straight line between the two. He had a bulging forehead, eyes that were too closely set, small, very dark, quick in their movements, and singularly piercing. Altogether, his was a face which the average man would find unprepossessing, and the physiognomist sinister. He was dressed untidily in a suit of flannels that had seen a good deal of wear. This carelessness of appearance was habitual, and was one of the many faults which his uncle found in him.

Stanley Bickershaw was celebrated as has been said. He was entitled to put a quite considerable proportion of the alphabet after his name, many of his degrees, however, having been conferred upon him by learned bodies as some appreciation of his distinguished services to the elucidation of hypnotic phenomena. His researches in the realm of hypnosis were vast, and much of the work he had done was unprecedented and upon lines entirely original. This was borne out by such publications of his as "Researches in the Subliminal," and "The Rationale of Hypnosis." Nevertheless, he remained poor, for hypnotism is hardly a marketable commodity; and whilst he won whole bushes of laurels, he made the disappointing discovery that the plant is a purely ornamental one incapable of bearing fruit of its own.

Consequently his appeals for assistance to his wealthy uncle were periodical; they recurred with the regularity of the seasons. Such an appeal had brought him to Herne Place on the afternoon with which we are concerned, and he took the very first opportunity—as soon as his uncle's man had ceased fussing with the tea-kettle and muffin-dish and had withdrawn—to broach the matter.

There was no necessity for him to enter into particulars; nor was he afforded the opportunity. From former experiences Orpington knew by Bickershaw's opening sentence precisely what was coming.

He sat up and dropped his eyeglass. "What? Again?" he exclaimed, a forbidding reproof in the question.

"I am sorry," said Bickershaw; but his tone was quite formal, his manner perfectly calm, conveying no hint of real regret. He was, as a matter of fact, deplorably lacking in any instincts of tact or diplomacy. His attitude towards the world was one of lofty contempt, of intolerance for a general ignorance which he was constantly flinging in its teeth. Looking upon his uncle as an integral part of that ignorant world which he despised, he was at no pains to dissemble his contempt even when seeking him on such an errand as the present one.

"I am sorry," he said then, "but progress is very gradual in the line I have chosen. The reward that should follow recognition is very slow in coming."

"That being the case," replied the practical uncle, "I recommend you to choose another line. What good are degrees if you won't turn them to account? Why don't you go into practice as a medical man? You're duly qualified."

"Oh, please!" said Bickershaw, with a quiet scorn that was magnificent, effacing the distasteful suggestion by a deprecatory movement of his broad hands. "I am not a practitioner. I am a scientist. You may not be able to appreciate the difference, but you may take my word for it that it exists."

"Obviously," snapped his uncle. "The one can make a living, and the other can't."

"Of course, if you are going to measure merit and achievement by the standard of a mere capacity for making money, then any tradesman is a better man than I am."

"He fulfils a more useful function in society."

"The matter is one that we will not argue. It is not given to some people to see beyond immediate returns. To them that by which a narrow community benefits at the moment is of more consequence than the labour by which humanity in general may benefit through centuries to come. I am afraid, my dear uncle, that you take that deplorable point of view."

Orpington screwed his glass into his eye, and scowled down upon his superior nephew. He set about returning him rudeness for rudeness, conviction for conviction.

"Your insufferable conceit," he said, "is an insuperable bar into your worldly success. Nothing else could lead you to imagine that the charlatanism and quackery which receives the applause of a few feeble-minded men and neurotic women is going to be of any benefit to humanity."

Bickershaw, entirely unruffled, smiled the lofty, tolerant smile that he reserved for ignorance too crass to merit the dignity of his scorn.

"I suppose you always consider people feeble-minded and neurotic when their notions of things do not happen to coincide with your own happy enlightenment."

"Quite so," said Orpington, intentionally provoking.

Bickershaw sighed. "I haven't your confidence—alas!"

"You've the confidence of Old Nick himself," snorted Orpington. A faint colour—reflex of his indignation—was stirring in his cheeks. "And it's just like your infernal impudence to come here and take this superior tone with the man from whom you're attempting to borrow money. What do you do with your money, anyway? You don't spend anything on clothes, as far as I can see; you're not man enough to have any dissipation; you're living at your cousin's and on your cousin; and I'm sure you don't gamble. Yet it's only three months since you had two hundred pounds from me. What do you do with it?"

Bickershaw produced a pipe, and proceeded calmly to load it. "You can't believe," he said, "how costly are my researches."

Orpington sneered.

"I am pursuing at the moment certain investigations," his nephew continued confidently, "substantiating certain theories which I have formed. I have arrived at the point where practical experiment is necessary, and for this I must have a medium. Now mediums are expensive. They demand large honorariums, and they have to be kept whilst the experiments are being conducted. These may last some time in my case. Now perhaps you understand."

"Pshaw!" was the rejoinder, undisguisedly contemptuous. "Empiricism of the rankest! Charlatanism! Neither more nor less. I was talking about it to Dr. Ross the other day when he came to see me about my indigestion, He says—"

"His opinion on such a subject," Bickershaw interrupted coolly, "is just about as valuable as your gardener's."

"He's a specialist," said Orpington.

"In gastric ailments—yes; just as your gardener is a specialist in gardens. I don't see that either is entitled to be considered an authority on hypnotic phenomena."

"Anyhow, he is able to make a living—and a jolly good one."

"We appear," replied Bickershaw, "to be arguing in a vicious circle. The point is—"

"The point is, will you earn your living if I put you in the way of doing so?"

"I desire nothing more ardently."

"Very well, then. I'll tell you what I'll do: I'll give you a thousand pounds to buy a practice."

For a moment Bickershaw's self-possession was shaken by disgust. He lighted his pipe and recovered. "Will you give me the thousand pounds without conditions?" he inquired with quiet impudence.

"No, I will not."

"Why not? What difference can it make to you? So long as you part with the money—"

"It will make this difference," was the answer. "If the money is put into a practice, and you know there is no more to come, you may work and keep yourself; whereas if you put it into this confounded hypnotic rot of yours, you'll be back again in six months, asking for more.

"Anyway, I've made you an offer. You can take it or leave it."

"You don't know what you are asking," Bickershaw protested. "Do you see me—me, Stanley Bickershaw—setting up as a general practitioner in some beastly suburb, spending my days and wasting my talents in treating young ladies for anaemia and old gentlemen for dyspepsia? Do you?"

The last remark was unfortunate, and it brought Anthony Orpington to his feet in a fine anger. He was

extremely sensitive on the score of his age, and he saw a
personal allusion to himself in the "old gentlemen with
dyspepsia."

"I think you'd better go, Stanley," he said, in the voice
of one who is exerting a heroic self-control. "You're
wasting your time here. I'm incapable, you know, of
following your mind into the fine shades of logic in
which it loves to meander. You have refused the only
offer I am likely to make you. I shall not repeat it. And
you may as well know that if you come pestering me any
more for money, I'll deprive you of the competence you
are to inherit under my will as it stands at present."

"But, my dear Uncle Anthony!" Bickershaw, too,
was on his feet, and belatedly he was attempting a
conciliatory tone, softening the scornful lines of his
mouth. "I assure you that I—"

"I don't give a durn for your assurances," was the
wrathful interruption. "You can go. I've said all that I am
going to say. And don't come near me again until you've
put your manners through a course of training. I'm done
with you, and I'm glad my poor sister isn't alive to see
the waster you've become."

The dismissal was final. Bickershaw picked up his
rather dingy straw hat. "Very well," he said. He recovered
something of his quiet insolence. "Sorry to have troubled
you," he added. "Good afternoon!" And he departed.

Two red spots of anger burned in his sallow cheeks;
yet through all his disappointment came a gleam of hope.
He was to benefit under his uncle's will; that was news
to him. A competence, his uncle had said; perhaps three
or four hundred a year; that would be his uncle's notion
of a competence. But the hopefulness of the outlook
was discounted when he came to consider his uncle's

extreme good health. Still, it was something to know that some day he would be in the enjoyment of an income that should insure him immunity from such pecuniary embarrassments as hampered him at every step. Meanwhile, however, there were his present considerable difficulties to be faced.

He considered the advisability of seeking assistance from his cousin, Major Francis Orpington, whose guest he was and had been now for some weeks past, and was likely to continue for an indefinite period.

He took his resolve upon that point, and stepped along more briskly despite the heat. He crossed the river at Romney Lock, and made his way along the towpath towards the Major's house at Old Windsor.

Coming up from the river, through the shrubbery he found Francis Orpington and the latter's sometime ward, Adelaide Burton, reclining in deck-chairs in the shade of a clump of trees on the edge of the tennis lawn. A racket lay on the grass beside Francis; he was in flannels and without a coat; there was a cigarette between his lips, and he held a long glass half-full of a beverage in which a piece of ice was floating. He was chatting gaily, and Adelaide was laughing as she listened, watching him with eyes full of affection—an affection by no means limited to what is due between ward and guardian.

Bickershaw, coming silently through the shrubbery, checked on the edge of the lawn, and stood quietly observing them, his presence unsuspected. There was no particular reason for his action. It was instinctive, a part of his rather warped nature, secretly to observe people. Had you charged him with spying or eavesdropping, it would probably have surprised him; yet, having considered your accusation, he would have brushed it aside as sentimental and frivolous.

So he stood there for a little while, considering them, listening to their lighthearted talk, and drawing conclusions of his own from what he heard and saw— fairly obvious conclusions, after all, which had none the less escaped his attention hitherto.

Major Francis Orpington was a younger edition of his uncle Anthony; he was tall, spare and active with the same high-bred, lean face, and the same habits of thought—which, no doubt, had much to do with the excellent relations that prevailed between himself and his uncle, whose acknowledged heir he was.

He was in his fortieth year, but he looked thirty, and felt twenty. And this, to some extent, may account for his having permitted himself to fall in love with his ward, notwithstanding that she was twelve years younger. Nevertheless, the consciousness of the disparity in age between himself and this daughter of his old friend, Edgar Burton—who for fifteen years now, ever since her father's death, had been under his tutelage—set a certain curb upon his feelings. So far it had prevented him from making a declaration which Adelaide very ardently desired.

At times he would toy tentatively with the question of her marrying, dangle it before her, use it as a plumb to sound the depths of her feelings and inform himself how far he might navigate his own barque upon these unknown waters which allured him and yet which he hesitated to explore, dreading shipwreck.

As if for the information of that silent watcher in the background, he was toying now with that momentous question.

"You're an impudent baggage, Adelaide," he told her, laughing. "You've no proper sort of respect for me. You forget at times that I'm your guardian; that I stand towards you *in loco parentis*, as it were."

"Your French is atrocious," she informed him.

"It happens to be Latin."

"You render both unintelligible."

"This is the most obvious and noisome of red herrings," he protested. "I am referring to your want of respect for me; your want of proper sense of the dignity of my position. It is high time I handed you over to a husband."

The mockery diminished in the brown eyes, the dark head was lowered for a moment; she studied her racket in silence. Then she laughed softly.

"If you imagine that you would thus impose obedience to a man upon me, you are hopelessly mistaken. It has gone out of fashion to obey a husband."

"And yet," said he, "in spite of that inducement to marry, you have remained single." He looked at her sideways as he spoke, his lips smiled, but his eyes had an anxious searching look.

"The right man never asked me," she answered, and faced him, laughing, almost challenging.

He turned his attention to his glass, and took a long pull through the straw. "There were suitors to spare in the old days," he said presently. "In fact, they became a confounded nuisance and a decided drain upon the resources of my modest establishment. They were a varied lot—no girl could have had a wider range of choice. And yet, like a brazen hussy you are, Adelaide, you encouraged them all, and married none. And now, when you're—let me see, how old is it safe to say you are?"

"Twenty," she answered shamelessly.

"To be sure, now that you're twenty, the suitors are not quite as plentiful, and you are still single; by no means blessedly single. Do you know, Adelaide, that you're a great disappointment to me? In whatever light I consider you—save perhaps as tennis-player—you're a failure."

She put out a hand, slender, strong and cool, and took him by the wrist. She looked up into his eyes, smiling gently and very alluringly. "Am I really such a disappointment to you, Frank?" she asked him.

Something of his mock-seriousness departed. He flung away his cigarette. A mild excitement fluttered through him. This was his hour. In the tide of his affairs of the heart, surely this was the flood. Upon its bosom, he would sail to fortune.

And then, whilst he was still pondering the words in which at last to launch his barque, a twig snapped behind them, and Stanley Bickershaw, sardonic and light-footed, stole like a snake into their Eden.

## II.

### THE CONTROL OF ADELAIDE

If Major Orpington was vexed by that interruption at the time of its occurrence, more deeply still was he vexed by it when he came, a week or so later, to view the matter in retrospect.

Not only did retrospection increase his assurance that the moment had been entirely favourable, but that it had been critically favourable—a moment which would not recur. For with each day that had sped there had seemed less chance of its recurring. Adelaide grew oddly reserved towards him; her manner became daily more distant.

This extraordinary change in her—this unaccountable ever-increasing aloofness—dated from the day after that upon which the Major had been so near to declaring himself; and he was intrigued to know whether the cause lay in her having suddenly instinctively guessed the declaration that had impended, or in a little difference that they had on the score of Bickershaw.

It had begun in a laughingly disparaging remark that he had made concerning his cousin's pursuits—for he very fully shared his uncle's opinion of them, and did not hesitate to set them down as so much clap-trap. It was by no means the first time that he had made such a remark to Adelaide, and it had never failed to draw an echoing laugh from her—but of a kindlier quality, in which tolerance and indulgence were blent with mockery. On this occasion, however, she did not respond to his humour by so much as a smile. The level brows were knit; the handsome dark face was overcast and brooding.

"Do you think you are quite fair to Stanley?" she inquired, her tone severe.

He was startled for a moment. Then he laughed. "Are you going to take up the cudgels for the magician?" he challenged her.

"I am not sure that it is right to mock at what we don't, perhaps, understand."

"It is intensely human," said he.

"That is the poorest excuse for shortcomings, just as it is the commonest. Of course, you haven't read any of Stanley's books."

He was astounded. "Have you?" he asked.

"I am reading 'Researches in the Subliminal' now. It is immensely interesting. It discovers for me how foolish and wilful people can be in their ignorance. The book is a revelation—an astounding revelation."

He walked along beside her in absolute silence for some moments. It was after breakfast, and they were pacing the lower end of the tennis-lawn, the Major pulling at his morning pipe. To say that her words and her tone amazed him would be very inadequately to express his feelings: his surprise, his irritation, his impatience, and a sense of lurking evil that began to haunt him.

"This is a very sudden change!" he said and he said it laughingly, to conceal his true feelings.

"Sudden changes of thought are inevitable when we have been content to take our opinions at second-hand," she answered didactically. "Until yesterday it is what I have been doing so far as Stanley and his work are concerned. Last night, for the first time in all these years, Stanley came and talked to me about himself. He impressed me by his sheer honesty and earnestness. I borrowed a copy of his 'Researches in the Subliminal,' and I am afraid that I sat up until very late. It is a book that holds you—a wonderful study."

"You should hear Uncle Anthony upon the subject."

"I am capable of forming opinions of my own, Frank," she answered loftily.

It was extraordinary. He considered her attentively, half-smiling still to disguise his seriousness, his positive and inexplicable anxiety. She bore his scrutiny with characteristic calm. Yes, it was extraordinary. This handsome, straight, clean-limbed young woman, who, though intelligent and cultured, could never have been called bookish, to be suddenly caught in the toils of such morbid clap-trap. He supposed women were like that; their emotional, sensation-loving natures were easily to be ensnared by the sort of thing of which Bickershaw was an exponent. But, somehow, he had accounted Adelaide different, more virile-minded, whilst no less womanly than the average of her sex. He did not pause to consider that Bickershaw's influence was one that made itself felt not only among women and neurotic men, but amongst eminent and learned scholars. He was satisfied that his own essentially material outlook was the only outlook possible to the healthy male.

It was from that moment as if between himself and Adelaide a chasm had suddenly split itself, a gulf that widened daily thereafter, until by the end of a week of brooding and positive unhappiness, which began to mar the equanimity of his amiable good-nature, he came to ask himself whether she were not falling in love with Bickershaw.

The notion was grotesque and incredible. He flung it off in scorn at first. Bickershaw, with his unhealthy face, his stoop, his pendulous nose and beady eyes, was a type that must be repulsive to women. Then there was his personal untidiness—an untidiness that bordered upon uncleanliness—his ill-made, dusty clothes ever baggy and threadbare at the knees, and his deadly cold, forbidding manner. Surely all this must be repellant to a girl of Adelaide's pronounced fastidiousness and healthy, open nature.

And yet the conviction gained upon him; it was not to be reasoned away; and the accompanying sense of evil increased. It was unquestionable that Bickershaw exerted a singular influence over those with whom he came into contact, despite his physical disadvantages. He seemed to exude some quality of compulsion. It was difficult to resist him when he desired anything. The Major himself had experienced this and had needed all his willpower and determination on more occasions than one when forced by his good sense to deny certain things to his cousin. The servants hated him, yet were more submissive to him than to the Major himself. In fact, one could not imagine—nor did it ever happen—that an inferior ever rebelled against Bickershaw's cold authority. More than once Orpington had actually seen an angry, snarling dog suddenly crouch down with a whimper of fear, trebling in every nerve under the stare of Bickershaw's beady eyes. Beyond doubt the man exerted an unnatural, uncanny masterfulness. And as the Major came to consider all this, and saw the daily changing demeanour of Adelaide, his uneasiness increased alarmingly.

Presently he was to have proof that his fears were by no means idle—that Bickershaw's influence over Adelaide was no figment of his imagination.

Bickershaw had appealed to him for help on the day after the fruitless visit to Anthony Orpington. The Major had refused. Necessity compelled him to do so. He reminded Bickershaw that he was far from wealthy, that he had need to exercise economy, and that beyond giving the latter a home, as he was doing, he was really unable to extend him any assistance.

He had experienced the usual difficulty, the usual diffidence in opposing his cousin. But he had been quite firm about it, and Bickershaw had not insisted. He had smiled quietly to himself, a little grimly, perhaps, as one who, driven by force of circumstances, decides upon a course he would otherwise have avoided.

And then, a week later, Adelaide came to Francis on morning when he was in his study, on an errand that startled him and afforded him the proof to which reference has been made.

She perched herself on the corner of his writing-table, as she had been in the habit of doing on such occasions for the past ten years. But the manner of doing it was very different from the usual.

"I want to help Stanley," she informed him quite abruptly. "He is urgently in need of money to carry on his researches. I want you to let me have a cheque for three hundred pounds, Frank. I suppose you can manage it."

He laid down his pen, and his keen, good-natured face was troubled. He looked straight before him through the window, considering his answer. Of course, Adelaide was her own mistress, and mistress of her own finances, although he had continued to control them for her ever since her majority, just as formerly. Her father had left her a modest fortune of some six hundred pounds a year, which under Francis's stewardship had considerably increased.

He looked at her keenly, and what he observed in her face did not reassure him. She was pale and rather tired-looking; her dark eyes, usually so keen and bright, looked dull, jaded, and vacant. Vacant! That was it. It was in all her face; not pronounced, perhaps, and only to be perceived by one who was familiar with her usual vivacity. But, unquestionably, it was there.

Francis Orpington's brows came together in an angry frown. This desire to assist Bickershaw with funds was the last straw; it was the proof of the hold the man was obtaining over her, and it was an unhealthy, evil hold, as her very countenance and the change it had undergone bore witness. It would not have needed his love for her to have stirred his anger now. He must in any case have detested her intimacy with such a man as his cousin. He made a swift examination of conscience, and he found no jealousy distorting his outlook. His anger was clean and honest, and dictated purely by his affection, by his concern for her.

At last he spoke, slowly, looking her straight between the eyes.

"Has Stanley asked you to help him?"

Her eyes fell. She fidgeted nervously with the buckle of her belt. And it was not like her to be nervous or to fidget; she was frankness and naturalness personified. "No," she said presently, "he has not."

"But he has hinted that it would be acceptable—hinted pretty broadly, eh?"

"You are really very unfair to him, Frank." Still her eyes avoided his. "He has not hinted—not exactly. He has simply told me in what straits he is for funds, and how it is embarrassing his work. There is nothing small or mean in his desire for money. He does not want it for himself, to waste it on pleasure as most men do. He wants to spend it in the interests of science and of humanity."

The Major's frown grew darker. He snorted impatiently. "Yes, I've heard him talk just like that. He must find you a singularly satisfactory disciple."

She flushed. "If you don't mind, Frank, I'd sooner not discuss it with you. You are so very much out of sympathy with Stanley. You don't understand him, and you take no interest in his work." She made the slightest pause. "You'll let me have that cheque today, won't you?"

He notice the change, the slight hardening of her tone, the altered choice of words which made of the thing a demand rather than a request. Of course, she was entirely within her rights.

"Certainly, if you wish it," he answered, and there was the least stiffening of his own tone and manner, for he was genuinely hurt. "The money's yours to dispose of as you please. At the same time, three hundred pounds is a considerable sum; as you realise, I suppose, that you stand very little chance of recovering it, once you lend it to Stanley."

"I don't mean to lend it. I intend it as a gift."

"As a gift? Oh!"

"Yes. I, too, should like to do something for—for the same cause. It's a little enough I can do. What is mere money, after all?"

"Oh, just rubbish, of course," said Francis, stung into sarcasm.

He opened a drawer and took out a cheque-book.

"If your mind is quite made up, I suppose there's no more to be said."

She didn't answer him; so he dipped his pen and wrote the desired cheque. "There you are," he said.

She took it, glanced over it, muttered a casual word of thanks and slipped off the table.

"Can you spare me five minutes?" he wondered. "I should like to have a talk with you, Adelaide."

"Not now," she put him off. "I can't at the moment. Later on, perhaps." And she left him.

He lay back in his chair, very thoughtful and very unhappy. He was unhappy about himself and about her. The change in her attitude towards him was so extraordinary, so complete. And the proof of his fears concerning Bickershaw's influence over her she had now afforded him—it was outrageous!

He sighed bitterly, and with knit brows slowly filled his pipe. He lighted it, and then slowly put it down.

Looking through the window he could see the far end of the tennis lawn, and there, on the edge of the shrubbery, she was pacing slowly with Bickershaw. She had refused him the five minutes he had begged of her that she might consecrate every moment of her spare time to his cousin.

He watched them, a very sullen anger in his heart. He observed that Bickershaw was talking; talking in that cold, impressive—horribly impressive—manner that he assumed when in earnest. The man's beady eyes scarcely left her face, and she, Orpington observed, returned his glance with one of wondering, admiring awe.

There was something abhorrent in the sight. Orpington could not define it, could not have said why it so impressed him. But it was there—something loathsome and evil that stirred his manhood and called loudly to his chivalry to hasten to the rescue.

At last he took a resolve. Bickershaw must go. There was no longer room for him in that house whose hospitality he was abusing.

"But how is he abusing it?" cried Conscience suddenly. And Orpington's honest nature stood appalled at what he believed to be his own meanness, from which such a suggestion had emanated—at the absurd jealousy that had deluded him.

That was it; he was jealous—a jealous old fool. And his jealousy was of so horrible and detestable a quality that he saw all manner of evil where none existed. Yet was it so? Again he made that examination of conscience; and this time he was left in doubt. He must bring a calm and impartial mind to give judgment upon the case. He would go and talk the matter over with Uncle Anthony. He went.

Anthony Orpington's judgment was brief and uncompromising.

"The fellow's a rotter, Frank. I'm done with him myself. Turn him out neck and crop."

The Major entered into the matter of his own feelings for Adelaide, taking his uncle into his confidence. He found Anthony—a confirmed misogynist—surprisingly sympathetic and approving.

"Why not? Why not? She'd be a fool to refuse you. I'm sure she's fond of you, and you know from experience that you can live in the same house without quarrelling. It isn't every prospective couple that has had the same chance of testing joint existence as you two have had. What's twelve years difference? Pooh! Marry her, and good luck to you."

Frank dwelt upon the signs of a change in her feelings towards him. His uncle dogmatized.

"All the more reason to get rid of the blackguard. He's at the bottom of it. Women swallow the sort of charlatanism he gives off as a baby swallows milk. Get rid of him."

"But that is just the point," Francis objected gloomily. "I am taking an unfair advantage. I am allowing my jealousy to dictate to my honesty. Stanley is rather in difficulties, and if I throw him over—"

"Serve him jolly well right," said the emphatic uncle. "Let me come and have a look at things."

"Oh, no, no."

"I'll walk over after lunch tomorrow if it's fine," Anthony insisted. "Expect me at about three."

The Major had gone to his uncle for advice; but like a good many people who in a quandary hesitate to take the only obvious course before them, he was none the better for it when he had received it. He returned home in the same frame of mind, in the same state of indecision.

He took the short cut that it was usual to take in walking from Herne Place; he crossed the river at Romney Lock, followed the towpath, and turned up into his own shrubbery. Through this, he came quite noiselessly by the pathway, where the soft, moist earth soundlessly received his footsteps. At the end of the lawn, just where this path debouched into it, stood a spacious summer-house, or rustic pavilion, that was in constant use. As Francis was passing this, he caught a sound that brought him instinctively to a standstill. It was the sound of a human voice—Bickershaw's voice, he realized presently—speaking in soft, curiously droning accents.

Puzzled, Francis stood listening; but he could distinguish no word of what was said; indeed, he was not sure that words were being uttered; rather did the sound, on closer acquaintance, seem like the crooning with which a mother lulls her child to sleep.

He approached, and looked through one of the windows. On a cane chaise-longue Adelaide was reclining in an attitude of intense fatigue, her hands folded on her lap, her bosom rising and falling with the steady rhythm of the sleeper, her face white and vacant to the point of ghastliness.

Before her sat Bickershaw, his little eyes malignantly agleam, his hands moving slowly down over her face and body, and then outwards and round again, his muttering those crooning sounds which had caught the Major's attention.

Francis Orpington may have had the slightest and most superficial acquaintance with the mysteries of hypnotism; but not for one second was he in doubt as to what was taking place in that pavilion.

It was as if a bandage had suddenly been plucked from the eyes of his mind. And subconsciously—without pausing to analyse his conclusions—he understood a host of things that had intrigued and mystified him in the last few days. But for this ocular proof of the manner in which Bickershaw was gaining his ascendancy over Adelaide, the Major would have laughed to scorn the very notion of any such influence being exerted, would have classed such stories with other old wives' tales of spooks and incantations.

But here he saw Bickershaw at work, and from what he saw realized at last the inexplicable, indefinable change in Adelaide, her aloofness from himself, her association with Bickershaw, the vacant expression he had observed in her countenance. Bickershaw had obtained control of her will, had rendered her the slave of his suggestions. The Major's strong skepticism withered on the instant, killed partly by the evidence before him, partly by very instinct.

He wrenched open the door of the summer-house and sprang into the little timbered chamber as if flung there by a catapult.

"You scoundrel!" he roared.

Bickershaw started up, and recoiled before the Major with a little whimper of fear, hands defensively raised, eyelids fluttering nervously. For Francis was truly terrific. His eyes blazed in his white face, and his hands were raised to strike.

He restrained himself, however. He took Adelaide by the shoulder and shook her roughly. A little moan was her only response; he turned on his cousin.

"Wake her," he commanded, his voice rasping. "Wake her instantly, or I'll smash you into pulp."

Unnerved, and very much afraid, Bickershaw obeyed at once. His voice was, nevertheless, quiet and cold. "Wake up, Adelaide," he said in tones that were perfectly conversational.

Obediently she stirred, the colour flowed gently back into her cheeks, and she opened her eyes. They were full of a bewilderment of one suddenly roused from sleep.

"Now come with me," the Major bade Bickershaw.

Bickershaw hesitated. He hung back, his lips tightened—the outward sign of a concentration of his will—and Francis found the man's beady eyes intently fixed on his own. It reminded him suddenly of Bickershaw's quelling of unruly dogs. But he was no poor brute to crouch down and whimper. The effrontery of the attempt to dominate him increased his anger. For an instant it overmastered him. He seized Bickershaw by the collar of his coat and shook him as a dog shakes a rat; then he flung him down the steps of the summer-house. He followed without another thought for Adelaide, slamming the door after him.

At the foot of the steps Bickershaw had recovered his balance. He saw the Major descending upon him like a thunderbolt. He edged aside out of the direct line of that descent.

"For Heaven's sake control yourself!" he cried, his voice commanding. "I—I can explain," he added weakly.

"You'll need to," was the grim answer. "Come with me." And taking him by the arm, Francis hurried him across the lawn towards the house.

## III.

## MAJOR ORPINGTON FALLS ASLEEP

Although Major Orpington recovered by an effort his outward composure, inwardly his anger continued to rage unabated. Nor could it abate whilst there abode with him the loathsome idea that Adelaide was in the monstrous power of his cousin. The picture of what he had seen in the summer-house persisted before the eyes of his mind and filled him with horror. And there was the thought that Adelaide—Adelaide, of all people—should have been a party to these abominable practices! It was monstrous, inconceivable!

So governed was he by his furious horror that when at last he found himself in the study with Bickershaw he had nothing to say. There were no words at the Major's command in which he could even begin to give expression to his feelings. And so, after a long, wrathful consideration of his cousin, he was forced to admit.

"I have nothing to say to you, after all. There are no words that will meet the case. It calls for deeds. I am tempted to thrash you—almost to kill you, I think. But—"he shrugged, snorting. "You had better go. Pack your things and leave my house at once, and never dare to enter it again."

By now Bickershaw had entirely recovered from his fright and was completely master of himself. His face wore an expression of regret. But through this, as through a thin veil, peeped the ineffaceable mockery habitual to his countenance. He moistened his lips before replying.

"You might, at least, first hear my explanation," he protested. "I don't quite know what you are imagining, Frank, but I am afraid you are doing me a very grave injustice. Of course, I will leave your house if you feel

like that about it; but I think I have the right to ask you
first to hear my case."

He played with consummate cunning upon the sense of
justice which he knew to be inherent in his cousin.

"Can you possibly find anything to say that will
mitigate the thing you have done?" There was as much
pain as anger in the question.

"A good deal. In the first place, there is the pecuniary
embarrassment in which I find myself."

Light blazed upon the Major's mind, and he wheeled
sharply upon his cousin, interrupting him.

"So you gained an ascendancy over Adelaide to induce
her to part with her money to you. That was how she
came to draw three hundred pounds for you. You made
her do it."

"Nothing of the sort," was the cold answer. And then
Bickershaw proceeded, lying boldly and cunningly with
just the lies he knew his cousin would believe. "Why,
you know yourself that all that is nonsense, that there is
no such thing as compelling a person to anything against
his will. That is the mere clap-trap of hypnotism, as you
know—as I have often heard you declare. The money
she lent me, she lent me of her own free will, because
she believes in me as a result of the talks we have had
together. Compulsion! Pshaw!"

He laughed the notion to scorn, and the Major began to
believe him, because it was the very thing he would have
hope, and because to believe it relieved him of more than
half his anxiety touching Adelaide.

"All that I did," Bickershaw pursued, "was to accept
Adelaide's very generous offer to supply the place of
the medium I was unable to afford. With the money she

insisted upon my accepting I need not have done this; but in her deep interest in the matter she was equally insistent upon that point. I was tempted by the discovery that she is gifted with quite exceptional mediumistic qualities, and I succumbed.

"But you do me more than an injustice if you suppose that I would have done this if it had been in any way hurtful. And as for my obtaining any control over her— why, it's a monstrous, foolish suggestion. I have done Adelaide not the slightest harm."

"No harm!" cried Francis. "Was there no harm in the thing I witnessed? Adelaide in a trance!"

"Well?" The coldness of the question had a singularly arresting effect. It seemed to demand the throwing over of prejudice, the opening of the mind to judgment after ignorance should be removed. "And what, after all, is a trance? It is sleep—just sleep. Hypnotism is nothing more."

"It is artificial," objected Francis, feeling rather at a loss.

"Oh, dear, no. Artificially induced, if you like, but not artificial in itself. I assure you again that I have done absolutely no harm. Still, in view of the deep-rooted objection arising from your imperfect knowledge of what the practice involves, I am quite prepared willingly to give you an undertaking never to repeat the experiments with Adelaide; but this merely as a concession to your prejudices, not as an admission that there is any harm in them."

"I can't believe you, Stanley. Adelaide has been different these last few days. Influences have been at work upon her."

"Granted. But why jump to conclusions about these influences? They are merely the influences of her newly acquired knowledge. Such influences as work upon every one of us on his way through life, and without which we should reach the grave much as we leave the cradle. To suggest that these influences have anything supernatural or occult—why—"he shrugged and laughed, contemptuously amused. "Surely you, Francis, of all men, are not going to harbor wild notions of that sort?"

The Major found himself at a loss what to think. After all, his old skepticism was more tenacious than for a moment it had seemed. "I did not mean exactly supernatural or occult," he muttered, frowning, utterly bewildered, for he feared that he had meant just that, and that he should not have meant it.

"Of what precisely do you accuse me, then?" cried Bickershaw, now master of the situation. "What evil can you suggest that I have done?"

Now, had Orpington not been in love with Adelaide, he might even at this stage have been firmer. It is odd that the very influence which should have strengthened his resolve to dismiss his cousin was the very influence that weakened it. For again, with that exceptional fairness and honesty of mind that was his own, he began to ask himself was he not perhaps doing his cousin an injustice, spurred by his jealousy to put an unnecessarily ugly construction upon the latter's relations with Adelaide.

Once he began to ask himself such questions he was lost. He still protested against the practices in which Bickershaw had indulged; but his protests became perfunctory, and Bickershaw met them in a deferential manner that was unusual in him, which, in itself, should have put the Major on his guard. For it was not Bickershaw's way to be meek or tolerant of the opinions of others where they conflicted with his own, unless he had ends to serve.

Thus it came about in the end that in view of Bickershaw's promise never to employ Adelaide as a medium; Francis consented to forget the matter.

Reflecting upon the whole affair later in the day, he was by no means sure that he had not been a sentimental ass, and weak out of an excessive sense of justice; for he found Adelaide more distant than ever in her bearings towards him. He reflected that if he had made a mistake Anthony Orpington would perhaps correct it on the morrow when he came over, which showed an increasing weakness on his part.

He announced his uncle's coming visit that night at dinner. Adelaide showed no interest in the announcement; but Bickershaw, after a spell of thoughtfulness, looked up casually to inquire at what time Anthony was expected.

"He said that he would come over immediately after lunch—at about three o'clock," replied the Major.

Bickershaw nodded, and lapsed into thought once more; but the subject of their uncle's visit was not pursued.

That night the Major slept very badly. In fact, he hardly slept at all. He was supremely unhappy on the score of Adelaide. The events of the day ran like a perpetual panorama before his eyes. Again and again he saw her reclining entranced in the chaise-longue in the summer-house, and he was filled anew with his original horror of the spectacle. Again and again he reproached himself for not having handled Bickershaw more firmly; he despised himself for it, in fact, and still more for his dependence upon his uncle to correct that error of judgment.

In the morning he had a scene with Adelaide that was almost angry—the first approach to an angry scene between them in all the fifteen years that she had resided under his roof. He had ventured to remonstrate mildly with her for having been a party to Stanley's experiments, and she had flown out at him; she had reproached him for being domineering, ignorant and dogmatic, and for interfering in her affairs, reminding him that she had long since passed from his tutelage, that she was a woman able to judge for herself, responsible to no one for her actions. She concluded with a hint that it was her intention to emancipate herself entirely from his supervision by making a home for herself elsewhere and soon.

It all hurt him very deeply. It was so unlike her; and in her harshness there had been something that had gone very near to ingratitude; for, after all, Francis had been her best friend since her father had died—father, brother, and everything else had he been to her.

She did not come to lunch. He and Bickershaw faced each other across the table and ate in silence. Francis drank a glass or two more than usual of claret, and this may have combined with his sleeplessness of the night before to render him presently drowsy and torpid. He took a book to the summer-house, flung himself down on the chaise-longue, and loaded his pipe.

Presently Bickershaw came in.

"Awfully hot," he said casually. "Cooler in here," he added, as if to explain his intrusion. He sat down and produced his own pipe.

The Major scarcely troubled to consider his cousin's easy effrontery under the existing circumstances. His drowsiness increased; his eyelids drooped, and he found reading a positive struggle. Then Bickershaw got up.

"I think I'll fetch a book, too," he said, and went out.

The movement roused the Major; for a few minutes he read on, consuming perhaps a couple of pages of his novel. Then Bickershaw returned, a book in his hand, and resumed his chair. The place settled down. Bickershaw was quite still. On the hot, languorous air a bee sailed in through the open window, humming soporifically.

Again Francis was nodding over his book, hypnotised by the white page and the black type with which he was struggling. Two or three times he recovered and strove valiantly to keep awake; on the last occasion he grew conscious that Bickershaw was regarding him with peculiar intentness out of his beady eyes. Francis's glance returned to his book, but the eyes seemed still there on the page before him, as we see on a white sheet the image of a flame at which we have looked. His torpor grew heavier, his breathing became regular, he lost his grip of consciousness and was asleep.

Sleeping thus, Francis Orpington was visited by a dream, curiously, singularly vivid in its detail.

He dreamt that he was there in that summer-house, sitting up in the chaise-longue, a prey to a strange excitement that was quickening his pulses.

He was slow in penetrating to the cause of this. The emotion that possessed him was not immediately to be defined.

In his hand he was balancing a heavy six-shooter, and as he perceived this the motive of his excitement gradually became clear. Anthony Orpington was coming soon to visit him. He was coming to interfere between Francis and Bickershaw; coming in his offhand, autocratic way to settle this troublesome matter of Adelaide and to settle it in a manner that was bound to be distasteful to the Major. That was his delusion, and he understood that his resolve was to prevent this at all costs.

His uncle must not see Adelaide or Bickershaw.

Francis must deal with him alone. His determination increased. It was an angry determination, a determination that would stop at nothing. He was filled by a frenzy, a fury of homicide. He would go down into the spinney, take cover, and wait until his uncle came. Then he would shoot him at close quarters, making sure to kill.

His course was now quite clear and definite. No thought of the consequences had any place in his dream. It carried him just as far as the shooting of his uncle. Not one step farther. All his mind, all his will, all his intelligence were focused upon just that point.

He dreamt that he rose from his seat, opened the door, and passed out of the little pavilion. He plunged into the spinney, avoiding the pathway, and making his way through the trees towards a certain point midway down between the lawn and the river. It was there that he would wait—there that he would do the thing. He moved with infinite care and without haste, for he had plenty of time. He gained at last the point that seemed in some way predetermined. He crouched there amid the tangled undergrowth to await his victim, the pistol ready in his hand, his homicidal frenzy increasing. The desire to kill, to shed blood, to destroy was overmastering. The contemplation of it filled him in anticipation with a sense of joy which he knew must reach its climax in realization.

But when again he came to consider that it was against his uncle—against Anthony Orpington—that his hand was to be raised, some of his joy perished. He dreamt that he set himself again to review the situation, and he found that he had been at fault in his earlier estimate of his uncle's intentions.

Whatever could have led him to suppose that Anthony Orpington's interference would be distasteful to himself?

He had been out of his senses. Anthony was coming because he himself had asked his help; he was coming to assist him to get rid of Bickershaw. Of course it was so. How had it been possible for him to forget that? When had his uncle ever crossed his wishes? They had always been the very best of friends; they had always understood each other as seldom happens between relatives of their degree. How, then, came he to be lying in wait for his best friend?

The wickedly joyous anticipation of the deed began to fade; a fierce struggle took place within his soul. His dream changed to the character of nightmare. He was oppressed, menaced by a deadly peril, in danger of perpetrating a loathsome deed. And suddenly he rebelled. The thing was absurd. If there was a man in the world against whom he should raise his weapon, upon whom he should vent the fury that possessed him, that man was Stanley Bickershaw—Bickershaw who was creeping like a snake between Adelaide and himself—Bickershaw who was destroying his peace of mind—Bickershaw who had been making horrible experiments with the soul of Adelaide.

Suddenly, in his dream, there came a crackle of steps in the undergrowth across the path. He felt his heart beating as if it would suffocate him. He crouched lower, until he was completely hidden behind a clump of laurels, and as he crouched the homicidal mania mounted again and overmastered him. He must kill. It was predestined that he must kill, and he would know no peace, no joy in life again until he had killed.

And then, quite suddenly, he became aware of a white, glistening face framed in the foliage beyond the path. The beady eyes were searching. It was borne in upon Francis that they were searching for him. They were the eyes of Bickershaw. Inaudibly the Major chuckled as he crouched still lower to baffle the search of those eyes.

And then the white face moved nearer. It seemed that below it there was a body—a human body. Of course there was; there was always, Orpington reflected, a body under a head. Besides, this was Bickershaw—Bickershaw standing there on the edge of the path, on tiptoe, peering about him, his livid face moist and gleaming.

Then it came to him again that it was Bickershaw who was his enemy, Bickershaw whom he hated. The homicidal frenzy surged up. It was Bickershaw whom he was to kill—Bickershaw, Bickershaw! The name boomed and boomed through his fevered brain. Of course, it was Bickershaw. However came he to imagine it was to have been his uncle?

He yielded to his furious, mad blood-lust. He rose and leapt forward from his hiding-place, leveling his pistol in the act so that the nozzle came within some few inches of his cousin's face. A second he paused, considering that livid face, the beady eyes suddenly less beady than he had ever known them—dilating widely in a curious, fearful fascination. Then he laughed, and pulled the trigger.

And on that Francis Orpington awoke.

## IV.

## THE AWAKENING

Francis Orpington awoke. A convulsive shudder ran through him, as it runs through those who are delivered from the thralldom of an evil dream. As the bonds of sleep dissolved themselves, and his awakening senses knew them for what they were, a great thankfulness welled up from the soul of him that this should have been no more than a dream.

And then, horror of horrors, worse horror than any that had been his throughout that nightmare, his thankfulness was checked in full flow, checked by complete consciousness of his surroundings. Although now awake, nothing was changed from what it had been in his dream.

He was standing there, under the trees in the spinney, on the identical spot where in his dream he had been standing. He saw the shadow-dappled sunshine at his feet, a little wisp of smoke hung at the height of his head, and before him, on the path's edge, protruding from the undergrowth, he beheld a pair of legs in grey, baggy trousers, the toes pointing heavenwards. A gap in the undergrowth showed where a body had crashed through.

His horror and amazement grew by leaps. A sense of bewilderment paralysed him. What had happened in this place? How came he there? And then the last thread of his half-formed impressions snapped, and he realized that his hand still clutched the heavy revolver of his dreams.

He considered it stupidly. How came he to be holding it? How came he to have fired it?

On that a fresh terror clutched him. If he had fired it, then—then that thing lying there was his handiwork. He rubbed his brow in a dazed, stupid fashion. He tried to think, and he came to the conclusion that he had not awakened when he imagined—that he was not yet awake at all—that the dream was continuing. But in dreams men do not dream that they have dreamt. The queer reflection leapt suddenly to his mind to increase its torture. But, then, it not still dreaming, how came he into such a position as this? And who was the man who lay there, half in, half out of the spinney?

He advanced a step or two to obtain a clear view of the face. The sight turned him almost sick with horror;

for the features were unrecognizable, so great was the disfigurement of the shot at such close quarters; but from the rest of the body he recognized beyond all doubt his cousin Stanley Bickershaw.

He felt as if an icy wind had suddenly enveloped him. On that sweltering July afternoon he was taken with a sudden chill; he was cold from head to foot, so cold that he shivered. Cold with horror and an unspeakable dread. For it was borne in upon his clearing senses that, however much of this awful affair might remain wrapped in mystery; one fact was clear: that he had killed Bickershaw, that he was a murderer.

He had been dreaming, he knew, and he had awakened; but he was no longer certain at what particular point in the sequel of events the awakening had taken place, for dream and awakening had followed each other in an unbroken, amazing continuity.

Dizzy and sick with horror he leaned against the bole of a tree, his eyes upon the disfigured face of the dead man. The pistol had slipped from his grasp, and lay unheeded by the dead man's hand.

What was he to do now?

Obviously there was but one course open to him as an honest, honourable man. He must give the alarm, make surrender to the authorities, and tell the true story of this inexplicable happening.

And swift upon the heels of that resolve came a fresh, fierce dread. The true story! The story of that somnambulistic dream! Tell a jury of sane, practical men that he had killed his cousin so? Why, it was ludicrous—grotesque. It must provoke the scorn of all right-minded folk. It would provoke their laughter but for the awfulness of the deed itself. Who in the world would believe so extravagant a story? It would be underlined in the annals of crime as the wildest and most impudent defence ever entered by a criminal. For he was a criminal—a murderer. He might not understand how the thing had come to pass; he might be quite certain that the thing had been done without volition of his own, and, therefore, that he was really innocent; but to the world, on the evidence of the facts—the only evidence the world would care about—he was a murderer, and as a murderer he would be hanged.

The thought stung him almost to anger. His outraged sense of innocence revolted at this aspect of his position. The more he insisted upon the truth of this matter, the more he would be treated as a shameless, foolish liar. The uprightness and honourableness of his past life would weigh for nothing in the scales of justice against such a tale as that.

Anthony Orpington would perhaps believe him mad. And Adelaide—what would she think? Why, surely, none would be more convinced of his guilt than she. Did she not know of his recent hostility to his cousin, of his threat to turn him out of the house, of his deep resentment on her own account?

It would not do. He dared not speak, dared not tell the world what he knew of Bickershaw's death. He must save himself by silence. So clamoured his reason, and his honour did not revolt. Since none would believe the story he had to tell, he would not tell it. He must play such a part as he would have played had he been the real murderer in intent as well as in fact, comforting himself with the knowledge that he had neither desired nor consciously procured the death of Bickershaw. He must protect himself by the only means in his power from the consequences of a deed of which his hand but not his mind was guilty.

This resolve taken, much of his calm returned. He
looked cautiously about; he listened intently. The deed
had had no witnesses. Nothing stirred.

He moved cautiously across the path again, and
plunged once more into the covert. Then he made his way
towards the summer-house, swiftly yet calmly watchful,
and pausing at every step to listen.

He gained the pavilion satisfied that he had not been
perceived. He closed the door, and flung himself heavily
down upon the chaise-longue, like a man exhausted.

If he had been cold before, he was burning now.
He mopped his brow, and lay back in his chair with
half-closed eyes. Again he reviewed the situation,
attempting to penetrate the fog of mystery in which it
was enveloped. His pipe lay on a little bamboo table at
his elbow, just where he had left it. By force of habit he
picked it up, and loaded it. He lighted it, and lay back to
give free reign to his speculation.

Suddenly he remembered the heavy pistol with which
he had shot his cousin. In the confusion of the moment,
in the half-paralysed state of his mind after the deed,
he had not bestowed a thought upon it. Now it recurred
to him, and the sudden recollection was almost like a
physical blow. Whence had that pistol come? Whose
was it? Not his. He owned no such pistol. He recollected
the weapon distinctly; it was unlike any that he had ever
possessed, and those that he did possess—his service
weapons—were all locked away upstairs. How, then, had
such a pistol come into his hands?

From that consideration it began to be borne in upon
him that the dream could by no means have ceased at
the point where he believed it to have ceased. It must
have continued long after the supposed awakening,

which must indeed, have been a part of the dream itself. For since such a pistol could not possibly have existed, neither could any other part of that horrible affair have been real.

Conviction grew. It must be so—no more than a strangely vivid, a strangely unpleasant dream, resulting from his overwrought state of mind and the extra glass of claret at lunch; and part of that dream was the slaying of Bickershaw and the slinking back into the summer-house. As a matter of fact, he had only just reawakened there where he had fallen asleep, and their unpleasant vividness in his waking moments had made him believe that such a series of events had actually taken place. It was often like that with dreams.

He breathed more freely. Much of the oppression was lifted from him. He became more and more convinced that he held the true explanation of the whole affair.

And then a shadow fell across the room, and a brisk contralto voice hailed him familiarly.

"Hallo, Frank! What have you done with Stanley?"

He jumped in sheer terror, and his movement was greeted by a burst of laughter from Adelaide, which it took him some moments to realise was reassuring.

"I declare you were asleep!" she mocked him. And her manner, as much as all the rest, filled him with a fresh amazement. For instead of the cold, aloof Adelaide of the past few days, who could scarcely find a civil word for him, here was the gay tease of a week ago restored to her habitual self.

Surely he was not awake even now. Here was but a fresh phase of this awful tormenting dream of his.

"You know," she continued, leaning her arms upon the sill of the open window, "you'll become obese if you indulge in these afternoon naps. And I should hate an obese guardian."

He smiled foolishly, vacantly. Words would not come to him in the depths of amazement into which he was plunged.

"But what have you done with Stanley?" she insisted. "He said he was coming here to read."

His course of deception began. "He was here," he answered; "but he must have gone out whilst I was asleep."

"I don't particularly want him. Only if you're too somnolent an old thing to come out and suffer defeat at croquet, I must find Stanley. He has the advantage of you in years, you know," she tormented him in the familiar way that had been so dear to him, and that he had so bitterly missed in these last few days.

He just stared at her, and thus provoked her fresh merriment.

"I really don't believe you're awake yet. I shall have to come inside and shake you. It won't do, you know."

Steps sounded, the quick steps of someone running up the path through the shrubbery. She turned to look, peered a moment, then gave a gasp of astonishment. "Why, it's Uncle Anthony," she cried. "Uncle Anthony running! He is being pursued at last by designing spinsters!"

But there was no smile on the Major's lips. A fresh fear gripped him by the heart. Anthony Orpington running! He had seen—— Then the thing was not a dream, after all. It was all real. Bickershaw lay down there, in the spinney, disfigured by a shot.

The elder Orpington came up, breathless but pale for all the exertion of running, and there was a curious horror in his eyes that at once struck the banter from Adelaide's lips. The Major rose, and crossed to the window. He must continue now to play the part he had chosen; the only part possible.

"Is Frank there?" he heard his uncle inquiring between gasps.

"Yes," answered Adelaide, "he's in here. Frank!" she turned to call. Then she questioned the elder man. "What's the matter? Has anything happened?"

He hesitated a moment. "Yes," he said. "I want to speak to Frank."

"Whatever is it?" asked Frank, from the window, his voice so calm and natural that it almost surprised him.

His uncle looked at him, and then at Adelaide. Obviously he was hesitating.

"Just run indoors, there's a good girl," he said. "I want to speak to Frank alone." And then, seeing her astonishment, he began to explain. "Fact is, there's been an accident. It's Bickershaw. I'm afraid he's—ah—rather badly hurt."

"Oh, poor Stanley!" she cried. There was a genuine concern in her tone, but nothing more—no transport of fear, no overwhelming anxiety, such as the Major who was watching her had been almost expecting. She scarcely changed colour; certainly no more than need any warm-hearted woman at hearing of an accident. How was this explainable? What had come to her? What had come to the world that afternoon?

The honest Major's bewilderment increased. For a week she had been more than friendly with Bickershaw, constantly in his company, taking up cudgels for him, and distant and haughty with the Major himself on Bickershaw's behalf. Yet here in the twinkling of an eye all was changed again; all was restored to the proportions that had been usual before Bickershaw had enlisted her sympathy some ten days ago. All this flashed through the Major's mind, to deepen its mystification, in the second between her expression of sympathy and his own eagerly uttered question:

"What is it?"

"You'd better just step down through the shrubbery with me," said his uncle. "Not you, Adelaide. Do run indoors, like a good girl. You'll know all about it presently."

From his grave face she saw that the matter was serious. "Stanley hasn't been killed, has he?"

The question was asked in a scared, strained voice. But no more scared or strained than was perfectly natural under the circumstances of what was feared by the speaker. Women do not find themselves beset by such suspicions without emotion. It is not in their nature, nor in man's, for that matter.

Anthony patted he shoulder. "Do go in the house," he said gravely; and it was an answer to her question as explicit as could have been given her.

The Major watched her closely. He heard her cry out, he heard her deeply pitying. "Oh, poor, poor Stanley!" He saw the glint of tears in her eyes, and approved it all; yet found it amazingly removed from what her recent relations with Bickershaw would have led him to expect.

He sprang out of the pavilion as she was making her way across the lawn towards the house. He caught his uncle by the arm.

"What is it?" he demanded, loathing himself for the deception he was forced to practice. "What has happened to him? Is he really dead?"

"He is down there," said Anthony, pointing with his cane, "lying half in, half out of the undergrowth, quite dead. He's shot himself—blown half his face away. The pistol's lying beside him. I've touched nothing, of course. Come down and see for yourself. It's perfectly horrible."

## V.

## THE CONFESSION

The conclusion to which Anthony Orpington had jumped at sight of Stanley Bickershaw's body, proved, after all, the same as that at which the jury arrived after a careful sifting of all the circumstances attending that gentleman's tragic end.

The police had gone fully into the matter, and they submitted their conclusions to the coroner. They had ferreted out that Bickershaw was very heavily involved in speculations, his losses amounting to close upon a thousand pounds—a matter which no one had suspected—and that he was absolutely without the means of paying. They had traced a gunsmith who recognized the revolver used as one which he had sold to Mr. Bickershaw a couple of months before, and who now deposed to that effect.

The medical evidence was rather neutral. The nature of the wound was by no means inconsistent, the medical witness held, with the theory that it was self-inflicted, although the revolver must have been held at a distance of four or five inches from the forehead, which was extremely unusual. Pressed, however, for a definite opinion, the doctor on the whole inclined to the belief that the deceased had shot himself. Then came Anthony Orpington, called to give evidence of the finding of the body. This he described in his clear, practical manner, adding the impression which he had instantly formed— the only tenable conclusion under the circumstances.

"Do you know," asked the coroner, "of any reason that might have led the deceased to take his own life?"

"I know of none beyond that discovered by the police," was the answer. "My nephew was certainly in financial difficulties. He had appealed to me for help some days before. I am afraid I was rather harsh with him. But, then, he made such a practice of obtaining funds from me that I was at the end of my patience. Nor was his way of asking, amounting practically to a demand, the best way of obtaining the assistance he sought. I not only refused to help him, but I threatened him that if he bothered me again I should cut him out of my will, under which he was to benefit by an annuity of two hundred and fifty pounds."

Finally, in the endeavor to clear up the last doubt, Major Orpington was called. He was perfectly calm and self-possessed when he entered his own dining-room, where the jury sat. He was the last person to have seen the deceased alive, and he was invited to submit the circumstances under which he had last so seen his cousin.

"I was in the pavilion in the garden after lunch," he deposed, "when my cousin joined me. He sat down and remained there for a few minutes; then he went out again, saying that he would fetch a book. He returned very shortly, and, in fact, he then had a book with him. I fancy we exchanged a remark or two, but I am not quite clear. I was very drowsy at the time. Soon after his return I must have fallen asleep. I awoke half an hour or so later, when Miss Burton roused me; and almost immediately afterwards my uncle ran up through the shrubbery with the news of what he had seen there as he passed through."

"You observed nothing unusual in the deceased's manner that day?"

"No. He seemed much as usual."

Asked did he know of his cousin's financial difficulties, witness replied that he knew of these difficulties, but not of their extent.

"He had applied to me for assistance, but I was not in a position to afford it. I gave him the hospitality of my house here, but beyond that I did not feel justified in going. I had, of course, no conception that he was in such straits as to be driven to so desperate an act. Nor did he at any time show any indication of it."

The end of it all was that the jury agreed that Stanley Bickershaw, harassed by his debts and driven to extremes by the attitude of his relatives—an attitude entirely justifiable, and nowise to be censured—had, in a fit of temporary insanity, committed suicide.

Nothing could have been more clear, and Major Orpington heaved a sigh of relief when he heard the verdict. The coroner came over to shake hands with him, and stood chatting for a few moments, the Major answering mechanically and absently to the remarks of this shrewd-eyed medico-legal gentleman. He was reflecting that were he now—or had he elected when called—to give the court the true facts of the case, they would treat him as insane, would regard him as the victim of an hallucination.

Indeed, there were moments in the days that followed when he did not know whether he should not so regard himself. Again and again he asked himself was he not labouring under some extraordinary delusion. He even went so far as to ask himself whether he had not been the sport of some freak of second sight, seeing in a dream an actual happening in which—after the inconsequent manner of dreams—he had imagined himself a participator.

The thing preyed upon his mind, haunted his memory by day and disturbed his nights with horrid visions. It became a recurrent dream of his that he was standing on the path in the spinney under the dappled shadow of the trees, peering at a pair of limp legs in baggy grey trousers that protruded from a tangle of undergrowth, the square toes pointing heavenward. And as he looked, the body behind those legs would heave itself up, topped by the mutilated face of Bickershaw, out of which Bickershaw's beady eyes glared maliciously, mockingly, menacingly. With a scream he would awaken and lie quivering in his bed, praying for daylight to dispel the chance of these horrors.

Naturally, his health began to suffer. He grew nervous and irritable under the awful strain, and he would sit for hours brooding over the matter, attempting to penetrate to the bottom of this mystery that was poisoning his existence. Had he or had he not killed Bickershaw? He no longer knew. The matter became more and more elusive. Unless light were thrown upon that dread mystery he feared, and with cause, that his reason would give way.

Adelaide he attempted to shun, but she would not be shunned. Her concern for him grew with his distemper. Her sincere affection for him manifested itself in a hundred thoughtful little ways that at another time would have filled him with thankfulness and joy, but which now served only to increase his ill-being. And then one evening, a fortnight after the inquest, she forced matters to a climax.

He was seated in a deck-chair on the lawn, near the pavilion, pulling moodily at his pipe, his brow gloomy, his mind black with ugly mystification, when she came gently behind him. She put her arms about his neck and laid her cheek against his in the affectionate manner that had persisted since the days when as a schoolgirl of fifteen she had first come to look upon him as a second father.

"Frank, dear," she murmured, "this awful affair of Stanley's is preying upon your mind. You are making yourself ill, and you are giving me a lot of anxiety. You need a change. You want to get away from this place. Supposing we were to go up to Scotland for a month. The sea-trout will be taking well on the Ythan, and in another fortnight the salmon will be running. Shall we go?"

Passionate angler as he was, the prospect tempted him. But his moral lassitude was such that the temptation could gain no hold. He sighed heavily, without answering.

She had dwelt much of late upon the things they had said on this very spot that evening, some six weeks ago now, and upon the declaration which she knew had then been trembling upon his lips, and which he must have uttered had not Bickershaw so inopportunely intruded. She loved Francis Orpington deeply and sincerely, and she had hoped and prayed that he might again find the courage to ask her to become his wife. Her quick, sensitive nature, so receptive of impressions, had long since perceived his diffidence, his fear that he was no longer of an age to be acceptable as a husband to her, his dread lest out of gratitude she should find it impossible to refuse him, and consequently his hesitation to place her in such a position by asking her.

That she read him aright she had never a doubt. She had helped and encouraged him to a declaration that evening six weeks ago. Since then the opportunity had never recurred, and in these last days she had been wondering whether perhaps that was not the matter that was preying upon his mind. Her pity for him, her sweet sympathy, her pure devotion urged her now to take her courage in both hands and force the situation.

"You need someone to take care of you, Frank dear," she murmured, a little breathless, a little pale.

He looked up at her and smiled gratefully; the smile irradiated, only to increase the wan, haggard look of his face. "I have you, Adelaide," he reminded her.

"Yes, but you never know," she answered with affected lightness, watching him intently as she spoke. "I might marry any day, and then what should you do?"

She saw the sudden frown, the darkening of the face, the painful twitch of his lips, and these signs filled her at once with pity and with joy. They were the signs for which she had hoped, and they gave her the necessary courage to proceed.

"Not that I want to leave you, Frank. There is no one like you. I could never care for anyone as I care for you. I could never be happy without you—never."

He turned quickly and looked at her very searchingly, a curious expression in his eyes, half doubt, half hope. Then he smiled.

"If I were a fool," he said slowly, "your words might tempt me to forget that you are my sometime ward and ask you to marry me."

"If you were fool enough to care for me, you mean, I suppose," she said, and she allowed her chagrin to manifest itself in her tone.

"I am," he answered, taken off his guard. "I do care. Adelaide, if—"

And then he stopped, his eyes fell, a crimson flush swept across his face, leaving it livid. "No, no," he cried. "Oh, I am mad—mad!"

She nestled closer to him. "Why?" she whispered, and then broke out, half resentful: "Must I do all the wooing, Frank? Are you to lead me on, to sound the depths of my feelings, and then to pause? Is that quite fair, do you think?"

His hand, hot as living fire, clutched her wrist a moment; his eyes blazed into her pale face. "Will you marry me, Adelaide—me?" he asked.

"Of course I will marry you, Frank. Whenever you wish."

"Oh, wait—wait!" He took his head in his hands and instant, his mind working fiercely. "Sit down," he said. "Forget what I have said—forget it until you hear what else I have to tell you. It—it is about Stanley Bickershaw."

She looked at him with dilating eyes. Alarm quivered through her soul. Already that quick receptivity of hers had caught more than a premonition of what was to come. She sank into the chair beside him, and took his hands in hers.

"What?" she asked breathlessly.

"I shot him," said the Major quietly.

She did not move; she made no sound; she just stared at him in silence, as if so great a fact needed time to penetrate in its entirety into her understanding. Then she nodded slowly.

"Yes," she said, her voice, too, curiously quiet. "Tell me about it."

A measure of relief was his already. It was as if he had flung off something of the burden that oppressed him. He went on more easily.

"I have told you the worst. I did not kill him intentionally."

"An accident?"

"I hardly know. Not quite an accident, I should say. Let me tell you." And quite quietly and naturally he told her the whole story. She listened intently, her brows knit, her mind all concentrated upon the points he made, following the narrative as a dog follows a spoor.

At the end she smiled wistfully, sympathetically. Hers was a fine, brave soul. "You did not kill him," she said. "You fired the pistol, but you were no more guilty than the pistol itself, since there was no intention on your part to kill, for you were not conscious at the time."

"But I was conscious," he reminded her.

"Yes, but your consciousness was a dream-consciousness, irresponsible, not guided by reason or will."

She grew very thoughtful. To doubt the exactness of his story never entered her mind. Nor did she suppose it an hallucination subsequent to the facts. It was all so clear, so perfectly circumstantial.

"Who shall say?" he cried almost fiercely. "Who will assure me that it was irresponsible? It seems so; it obviously is so; and yet—and yet—the thing remains with me, crushing, haunting, torturing. I remember that in those days I had come to hate Bickershaw, for he seemed to have come between you and me."

"Stanley?" she questioned. "Came between you and me? What are you saying, Frank? When?"

"When? Why, in those days immediately before his death, when you grew so very distant with me; when your every thought and every moment of your time were for him."

"Frank!" It was an exclamation of utter astonishment; and then her brows were knit and her eyes grew very thoughtful. Evidently his words had touched some chord of memory—dim and elusive, yet of a presence not to be ignored. "I do seem to remember something of the sort," she murmured. "Odd!" Slowly her face grew very white. "I wonder!" she cried, clenching her hands. "I wonder!"

"What?" he inquired.

"Nothing. Go on. You were saying how he seemed to have come between us."

"Why, yes. I had come to hate him for it. I may have willed his death; and in a dream state I may have carried out the desires of my subconsciousness. Oh, I don't know. I don't understand these things. I have looked upon it all as so much empiricism, so much quackery to impose upon fools. And now I begin to fear, actually to fear, that I may have been wrong; that there may, after all, be something in the theories that Bickershaw expounded."

"I understand," she said slowly. "I can see exactly what is torturing you, Frank. You are in darkness—a terrifying darkness, and you crave light."

"That's it. I am like a child in the dark—afraid, horribly afraid. It is the mystification of it all that is preying upon my mind and driving me mad. If that darkness were dispelled—— But who is there that can dispel it?"

"I think I know," she answered. "Have you ever heard of Dr. Galliphant?"

"I have heard of him, of course. An occultist, isn't he?"

"I suppose that is what people call him. But there is very little that is occult about him. He rationalises everything connected with what is known as supernal phenomena. In his hands the occult ceases to be occult; he reasons it out, reduces it almost to a material condition. What he cannot so treat he does not touch. He is the most eminent authority on hypnotism—living or dead. Bickershaw almost worshipped him, slightly though he knew him."

"But what can he do for me?" asked the Major, and there was a tinge of scorn in his voice; for convictions die hard, and the Major was reluctant to admit that a man of such pursuits could exist without being an empiric.

"I don't know. Perhaps nothing; perhaps much. It all depends where the evil lies, what the evil is. That, at least, he will soon tell you. Let me write to him."

"Do you know him?"

"No; but I now his books. Stanley gave me them to read. Besides, he knows Stanley's work, and if I mentioned that I wished to consult him—that you wished to consult him concerning certain very curious matters in connection with Stanley's death, he would come at once. He is not a professional occultist, you know. He is a man who is devoting his life and fortune to the elucidation of these phenomena and to the exposure of impostors."

Nothing that she could have said could better have commended Galliphant to Orpington. Yet still he hesitated.

"How much must I tell him?" he asked, alarmed, and added: "For we must be prepared for his unbelief of the mysterious part of it; he may jump at the conclusion that there has been just a vulgar murder and nothing more."

She shook her head confidently. "Have no fear of that. If you were a murderer, yes. But you are not, you know. And Galliphant will soon perceive that. No fraud could impose upon him; neither could a truth remain hidden where complete frankness is used. Let me write to him, Frank."

Her hand closed over his, and pressed it gently, coaxingly. He gave way; and having done so, he became infected by something of her own faith in this famous man who was but a name to him, and his case seemed suddenly more hopeful.

For some little time they remained chatting there in soft undertones, seeking for hope that this dreadful mystery would not bring another tragedy in its train.

It was dusk by now. They rose, and went indoors; and she wrote her letter there and then, fearful lest the Major should change his mind and revert to his old antipathy for all connected with the occult.

## VI.

### DR. GALLIPHANT

Just after lunch the next day, and whilst that were still at table, the butler presented to his master a salver which bore a card on which the Major read the name of Dr. Roger Galliphant. He took it up slowly, fingered it uneasily a moment, frowning, hesitation and dread again pervading him.

"The gentleman is waiting in the library, sir," the butler said.

He nodded mechanically. "Thanks, Smith. I'll be there in a moment."

The butler withdrew.

"It is Dr. Galliphant, is it not?" said Adelaide, faintly excited.

"Yes." Orpington rose. "I suppose we must go through with it now. You'll come, won't you, Adelaide?"

"Certainly, if you wish it."

They found him waiting in the library, as the butler had said; and at first glance the Major was more than favourably impressed by the tall, slender, well-groomed man who stepped forward to introduce himself. His hair, which was thick and slightly wavy about the temples, was almost snow-white, giving one at first the impression that here was an old man. But a glance at the young tanned face beneath, and the keen eyes, large, and of a singularly deep blue, corrected the impression, and led people to believe Galliphant even younger than he really was. He had a deep, pleasant voice, and his tones were level and soothing; his smile was a revelation of kindliness that was entirely irresistible, and he smiled now as he asked to be informed in what he could be of service.

The Major began with apologies for troubling him. These Galliphant cut short, placing all the obligation of the affair on his own side with a courteousness that was entirely charming. There was a subtle quality in his air and manner that set the Major more and more at his ease, invited his confidence, indeed, made him come to desire to confide in one whose sympathies were so manifestly ready.

They sat down, and the Major told his story, precisely as he had told it last night to Adelaide. Galliphant heard him attentively with a face that was as dispassionate, as inscrutable as a mask. The murder left him entirely cold. He was not considering it as an act of violence, but a part of a problem to which he was desired to apply his knowledge and his intellect.

When the Major had concluded—concluded at the point where Adelaide had come to the window of the summer-house—Galliphant continued quite still and thoughtful for some moments. At last he spoke.

"Most interesting," was his comment. "Indeed, I might say, quite extraordinary. I do not think that I have ever come upon a case that even remotely resembles it. Bickershaw, I know, had certain theories—dangerous theories. I rather think they have recoiled upon him. It is highly perilous to unchain forces which we cannot be sure of entirely controlling."

"Then—then," cried the Major, "you see light! You can penetrate this riddle?"

"Sufficiently, I think, to be able unreservedly to say that you have been very wickedly abused, and most certainly that you are in no sense guilty of murder, conscious or unconscious."

"Conscious or unconscious!" echoed the Major. "But is it an hallucination, then—the whole thing?"

Galliphant shook his head, smiling faintly. He rose. "I hesitate to express my opinion just yet. I should first like an independent confirmation of my theory."

"An independent confirmation? But how is that possible?"

"Why, by means of clairvoyance. If I were to induce a good medium into a trance, and place him *en rapport* with you—"

"The medium is here, Dr. Galliphant," said Adelaide, rising.

Orpington, at once understanding her intention, made haste to protest.

"No, no, Adelaide. Not that—please!"

Galliphant held himself aloof from the threatened discussion.

"Why not?" said Adelaide. "Since it is necessary, who better that I for the purpose?"

The Major clenched his hands. "But it is a dreadful condition. I saw you in that state when Bickershaw hypnotised you, remember; and the horror of it remained with me for days."

Galliphant's eyes narrowed suddenly. "Bickershaw used you as a medium, did he, Miss Burton?" he inquired. "Was this just before your close association with him of which Major Orpington has told us—which gave rise to those feelings which he fears might subconsciously have impelled him to take Bickershaw's life?"

Her brows were knit. She had grown quite white. "Really, Dr. Galliphant," she said, "my recollection of this close association is singularly faint. It exists, I admit. It was evoked by Major Orpington's mentioning it last night. But it exists rather as a dream-memory. I remember quite clearly that he interested me in his work and induced me to become his medium. But the rest is very vague and misty."

"Quite so," said Galliphant, his tone very full of understanding. "Quite so. Tell me, Major Orpington, you no doubt observed a sudden change in Miss Burton immediately after Bickershaw's decease? I take it, she would be more like her normal self—what she had been before she assisted him in his experiments, eh?"

"That is indeed so. It amazed me. It was one of the most amazing features of this case. But how did you come to know of it?"

"Oh, it is perfectly plain that Bickershaw had obtained a control over her. In her waking state she obeyed the suggestions he made to her during hypnosis. His hold would become stronger each time he hypnotised her."

"Oh, surely, surely not!" she cried.

"How do you yourself explain your having made him a present of three hundred pounds?" asked Galliphant, bending his keen eyes upon her.

"Really," she faltered, "I am afraid you are quite right. I could not explain it. I hoped it arose from a transitory infatuation with the subject of hypnotism."

"Say, rather, a transitory subjection to Bickershaw's will, Miss Burton. That is the correct explanation. A subjection transitory because, fortunately for you, he met his death when he did, thus dissolving the bonds by which he held you."

She sat down, and covered her face with her hands. "I have been afraid to think of it," she admitted. "But that is precisely what I had begun to fear."

"I think, Major Orpington, you would do well to avail yourself of Miss Burton's offer of assistance to unravel this tangle for you."

She sprang up, too, "I think we are wasting Dr. Galliphant's time," she said gently. "By all means let me submit. He will find me a ready medium, I believe, easily to be induced. And it shall be for the last time—absolutely."

Orpington gave way, and at Galliphant's invitation Adelaide seated herself with her back to a window through which the sun was shining. On the arm of her chair, the sunlight full in his face, Galliphant took his seat.

"Please sit over there, Major, out of her line of vision, so that you will not distract her. Now, please look at me, Miss Burton."

He employed no method but that known as fascination. His bright eyes riveted themselves upon hers, and steadily held her glance for a couple of long minutes that seemed an hour to the uneasy Major. At the end of that little spell came the first droop, the first sign of heaviness to her eyelids. And now Galliphant very gently raised his hands, and made long, slow downward passes over her.

"So," he murmured, his voice caressing, droning. "So! Go to sleep! Go to sleep—to sleep—sleep! 'Sh-h!"

With a long, shuddering sigh she sank back into the easy chair, her breath regular, asleep.

The operator rose, and stepped back. "An excellent subject," he commented quite casually, smiling reassuringly at the Major.

He placed a chair to face the sleeping woman, and summoned Orpington.

"Sit here, Major. Now, take her hands. Hold them firmly, but not too firmly. That's it. Now concentrate your mind as fully as you are able upon the scene of Bickershaw's death. Endeavour to visualise it again."

He stepped round to Adelaide's side and placed his hand on her brow.

"You hear me, Miss Burton, don't you?" he said.

The lips of the sleeper parted. There was a pause. Then a faint "Yes" fluttered through.

"Do you see anything?" inquired the operator.

"I see the spinney, between the lawn and the river," she replied. "There are two men there, one on either side of the path, among the trees. They are approaching each other. They are watching each other. Both are moving very carefully. One of them comes forward out of the trees. It is Stanley Bickershaw. Now the other leaps suddenly towards him. He raises a pistol. He thrusts it almost into Stanley's face—"

"Wait!" rang the sharp command from Galliphant. "Who is this man with the pistol? Look at his face, and tell me."

There was a pause. The medium's breathing was quickened, her brows were knit, her lip trembled, perspiration stood in beads upon her pale forehead; every line of her betokened a terrible exertion. At last she spoke, falteringly: "I cannot see it. It is very faint, very blurred and indistinct."

"Concentrate you attention upon that face, Miss Burton," Galliphant insisted. "You must see it, and tell me whose it is."

The signs of exertion increased. At last the tension was eased. "I see!" she cried. "It is Stanley Bickershaw's face. There are two Stanleys there."

"Now go on," said Galliphant.

"He—this other Bickershaw fires the pistol, and the first one falls back among the shrubs."

Galliphant's hand left her brow. He touched her lightly on the shoulder.

"Wake up, Miss Burton," he commanded sharply, and almost instantly her eyes opened, and she sat up. "That is all we require," he explained to Orpington.

The Major gasped. "But what does it mean?" he cried, more bewildered than ever.

"Could anything be plainer?" asked Galliphant. He was gently rubbing his hands, his satisfied smile showing that the medium's vision had confirmed his theories. He turned to Miss Burton and repeated for her precisely what in her trance she had told them. "Do you see light, Miss Burton?" he inquired.

"But, surely," she answered, puzzled, "the only possible meaning is that Stanley committed suicide. Stanley shot Stanley."

"True. But remember that although both had the same face, yet there actually were two men there, acting differently—Bickershaw and another. The other's face was blurred to you at first, not clearly visible. Yet you are quite right; it was Bickershaw who killed Bickershaw; yet it was not suicide. I should call it death by misadventure. The truth, Major, is that Bickershaw hypnotised you and willed you to do a murder."

"Hypnotised me?" cried the Major. "I can assure you that he did not."

"The facts prove otherwise. You may have no suspicion of it; but he hypnotised you none the less."

"How is that possible? Can such things be?"

"Bickershaw believed it possible, and to an extent has proved it possible in your own case. But we'll come to the manner of it presently. First let me relate the story of the event precisely as I now know it to have occurred."

He took a seat near the window. "Briefly, then, this is what happened: Bickershaw learnt at his interview with his uncle that by the latter's will he would benefit to the extent of a yearly competence. Along what track of thought that consideration started him it would be idle to speculate. But certain it is that he determined to improve his chances, and not only to inherit more than his uncle had provided—by removing his co-heir, yourself—but to inherit at once. To this monstrous end of his, he gains a control over you that afternoon in the pavilion. Anthony Orpington is expected presently. He has said that he will walk over, and no doubt he will come by the usual way—along the tow-path and up through the spinney. Bickershaw imposes his will upon you. He puts a pistol in your hand, and sends you to meet your uncle and to shoot him—and to shoot him at close quarters, making sure to kill.

"Thus removing his uncle and his cousin—the one by murder, the other as the murderer—Bickershaw not only revenges himself upon you both for your indifference to his wants, but, being the next of kin, he is enriched and cleared of his difficulties. The plan was diabolical in its subtle simplicity. Its one flaw was the pistol. But Bickershaw was driven to act on the spur of the moment almost, and had not time to possess himself of one of your own weapons. The subsequent explanation, had you shot your uncle, would no doubt have been that you had taken Bickershaw's pistol as being the only one at hand.

"Remember now your dream. You were imbued with homicidal mania, but you revolted when you found that it was directed against your uncle. That resulted from Bickershaw's control of you being imperfect, incomplete. He had succeeded in instilling the homicidal frenzy into your mind. But when he attempted to direct it against a person esteemed by you, he failed. Loosely controlled as you were, you obeyed the homicidal suggestion, but you followed, as it were, your own inclinations in the matter— your own controlling mind—and you vented it upon the one man you had cause to dislike and distrust, upon Bickershaw himself—who had been so rash as to be at hand, no doubt out of his anxiety to see the result of an experiment of which he was anything but sure."

"My God! How perfectly horrible!" cried the Major.

"But how perfectly just—how divinely just was the recoil that caught him in his own springe! You see now, do you not, how perfectly logical are these conclusions, how absolutely obvious, especially in the light of the confirmation afforded by Miss Burton, who saw not you, but Bickershaw himself as the slayer."

"Why?" asked Orpington. "Why did she see Bickershaw, since it was I?"

"But it was *not* you," Galliphant objected. "It was Bickershaw. You must remember that a medium does not see things with physical eyes. The medium's mind, in a super-sensitive, acute state of receptivity, absorbs the impressions of other minds; and the mind, the will at the back of your deed was Bickershaw's; therefore it was of Bickershaw that Miss Burton received an impression— blurred and indistinct at first, precisely because it blent with an impression of your own personality."

The Major rose to his feet. A man at all times reserved and undemonstrative, he was, nevertheless, so moved in the immensity of his relief that he gave way to impulse. He seized hold of both of Galliphant's hands and pressed them warmly.

"I don't know what to say, how to thank you. My nightmare is at an end. You have shown me that the finding of the jury was substantially correct, or that if it erred, it erred in mercy to the memory of Bickershaw." Then he paused, and some of his confidence left him. "But you have not yet told me how Bickershaw obtained this—this control, as you call it."

Galliphant crossed to one of the bookshelves. "Bickershaw himself shall explain that for you," he said. "I observed this volume whilst I was waiting for you."

He took down a black-bound copy of Bickershaw's "Rationale of Hypnosis," turned to the index, found what he sought, and opened the book at the page indicated. "Let me read you this passage:

"'Hypnosis, properly speaking, is no more than sleep, although artificially induced. The unconsciousness which supervenes is gradual; it has distinct stages, the first of which is the withdrawal of the will-power. That moment, before the subconscious faculties have ceased their activities, is the moment of control; the moment when the hypnotist thrusts in his own will to replace that of the slumberer, and obtains, as it were, a grip of his subject's mental part. The grip will be more or less firm according to the mediumistic powers of the subject.

"Now the fact not generally recognized is that this moment of control occurs alike whether the sleep is a natural one or the artificially induced one that we call hypnosis; and the operator who is experienced enough to judge with accuracy when that moment has arrived and to seize the chance it offers him, may obtain as complete a control of the sleeper as if the sleep itself had been hypnotically induced by him. It is for him to suggest in that moment and the control is obtained.

"Who has not fallen a victim to the suggestion of the knock upon his door with which he is awakened in the morning? We all know what dreams it has evoked for us—dreams in which that knock is the controlling power. Conceive, then, from that what must happen if a calculated suggestion is made by a skilled operator at such a moment.'"

Galliphant closed the book. "Now you will understand," he said. "It was a theory of Bickershaw's which received a good deal of adverse criticism at the time it was propounded. He would never have had recourse to it if any other way had offered for obtaining the desired control of you. But there was no other way; and so he adopted this, and risked its dangers."

"I understand," cried Orpington; and then he smiled bitterly. "If ever a man was punished for skepticism, I am that man."

With that he would have further expressed his deep sense of gratitude but that Galliphant stayed him.

"It has been profoundly interesting," he assured the Major; "the most interesting problem I have been asked to unravel. Also I have derived not a little instruction from this one instance—the only one on record, I believe—of the application of Bickershaw's theory touching his 'moment of control.' It quite confirms my own opinion of it, which is gratifying. And I am glad, too, to have been of service to you, Major Orpington. I need hardly say that in this matter I shall observe the secrecy of the confessional."

When the eminent occultist had departed, Major Orpington and Adelaide confronted each other in the library. He took her hand. She smiled, and attempted lightness.

"Well?" she asked. "Is it to be Scotland and the sea-trout?"

Before he could answer her she was in tears. He took her in his arms.

"If you'll marry me, Adelaide," he said, "I care very little where the honeymoon is spent."

# Review of *The Recoil*, a Film Adaptation of *The Dream*

The following review appeared in the April 3, 1922 issue of *The Times* of London:

"The most interesting of the films shown to the trade last week, was *The Recoil*, an adaptation of Mr. Rafael Sabatini's novel, *The Dream*, which is the work of the Hardy Film Company. It is being issued to the public by the Stoll firm. The most distinctive fact about this film is that it was adapted for the screen by its own author. That is a great advantage. There have been so many examples recently of novels that have been transformed into films by unsympathetic hands that it is pleasing to find an author who has sufficient regard for his own creations to take the responsibility of redressing them to fit their new environment.

Mr. Sabatini has certainly done very much better than the professional adapter of novels. Indeed, he makes out of his story a better film play than novel. The plot of *The Recoil* is built up on the foundation of hypnotism. The villain is learned in that lore and whenever he wants to achieve his wicked ends he resorts to it. First of all he influences the heroine, charmingly played by Miss Phyllis Titmuss. He makes her fall in love with him—to the annoyance of her fiancé, the hero (Mr. Eille Norwood). Then to deal with the hero he hypnotizes him and orders him to kill a mutual relation (Mr. Dawson

Milward). The hero does his best to oblige, but by the end of several thousand feet of film the villain's hypnotic powers seem to have waned, for the hero obeys the impulse but kills the wrong person. He slays the villain. That, of course, solves all the difficulties. The heroine at once emerges from her trance and marries the hero, and the mutual relation blesses the union with smiles and financial help. It all makes a successful film, thanks partly to the efforts of its author as a scenario writer, partly to the actors and actresses, who all play exceedingly well, and partly to Mr. Geoffrey Malins, the producer. *The Recoil* is not so good as *Bluff*, the preceding production by the Hardy Film Company, but it is a good deal above the average and should be very popular. A word of praise should be given to the sub-titles and letterpress of this film. They are all in excellent English and impeccable taste."

[Note: *The Recoil* was made during the silent film era.]

# Also Available...

**_Death by Suggestion_** _gathers together_ twenty-two stories from the 19th and early 20th century where hypnotism is used to cause death—either intentionally or by accident. Revenge is a motive for many of the stories, but this anthology also contains tales where characters die because they have a suicide wish, or they need to kill an abusive or unwanted spouse, or they just really enjoy inflicting pain on others. This volume also includes an introduction which provides a brief history of hypnotism as well as a listing of real-life cases where the use of hypnotism led to (or allegedly led to) death.— Back cover

"_Donald K. Hartman's DEATH BY SUGGESTION, is a melange of crime fiction featuring stabbings, clifftop suicides, hangings and the odd strangulation. Hartman offers an admirable introduction, exploring the history of hypnotism and defining the terms 'mesmerism' and 'hypnotism.' He discusses the positive and negative applications of hypnotism today before looking at modern criminal cases as well as those well-reported cases relating to his selection of stories._"

—TIMES LITERARY SUPPLEMENT, January 15, 2019, p.30

_Available from_
Amazon and Barnes & Noble
_in print and on Kindle_

This is the second volume in the "Hypnotism in Victorian and Edwardian Era Fiction" series, published by Themes & Settings in Fiction Press. The two stories collected here were published during the time of the Jack the Ripper killings, and they are among the earliest fictional accounts dealing with the Whitechapel murders. Both of these stories have Jack the Ripper being an American, who travelled from New York City to London to commit the murders, and the Ripper commits his crimes while under the influence of hypnotism. The first story, "The Whitechapel Mystery; A Psychological Problem

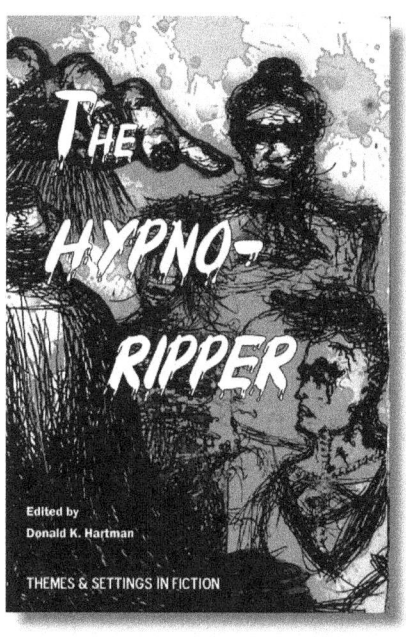

("Jack the Ripper")," is a novel authored by N. T. Oliver, and originally published in 1889 by the Eagle Publishing Company. The second story, "The Whitechapel Horrors," is a short tale, published anonymously in two American newspapers, shortly after the murder of Mary Jane Kelly in November 1888. Also included is a lengthy biographical profile on Edward Oliver Tilburn. "N. T. Oliver" was a pseudonym for the highly interesting Edward Oliver Tilburn. Besides being an author, Tilburn was a minister, actor, lecturer, secretary for several cities' Chambers of Commerce, snake-oil salesman, Christian psychologist, as well as an accused embezzler, shady real estate broker, and a self-proclaimed medical doctor.

Available from
Amazon and Barnes & Noble
in print and on Kindle

# Also

**What do you get when you combine "Buffalo Bill" Cody with Bernie Madoff, and for good measure throw in an actor, a cookbook author, a college founder, a faith-healer, an embezzler, and a bigamist?**

**Answer: Edward Oliver Tilburn**

E.O. Tilburn (aka N.T. Oliver, Ned Oliver, and Nevada Ned) was a late 19th/early 20th century con-artist that has somehow flown under the radar of both biographers and historians, but in this book Donald Hartman has revealed Tilburn to the world, and his life story should be of interest to folks that are fascinated by con men, as well as to those readers that enjoy getting a glimpse into the lives of scoundrels and frauds.

Hartman included a biographical profile on Tilburn in *The Hypno-Ripper* and the *BlueInk Review* says, "However, the highlight of the book is Hartman's 40-page biography of Oliver. The editor's meticulous research enables him to engross readers with the true story of this part-time author, snake-oil salesman, minister, faith healer, medicine show barker, sharp shooter, real estate mogul, city commissioner and, likely, bigamist—proving that, indeed, truth is sometimes stranger than fiction."

Jason Half commented on the same work, "In the book's final section, Hartman provides a fascinating and well-researched biography of Tilburn, alias N.T. Oliver and "Nevada Ned", and the man's rollercoaster of a life does not disappoint. In sum, Tilburn – sometimes with an "E" at the end of his name, sometimes not, but usually with an unearned honorific like "Dr." or "Ph.D." attached – was a patent medicine huckster, an author, a preacher, a professor, a realtor, and a man of business to the American towns and people he would descend upon, swindle, and leave."

*Available from*
Amazon and Barnes & Noble
*in print and on Kindle*